PRAISE FOR THE NOVELS OF STEPHANIE HANSEN

"Young adults seeking sci-fi stories about personal and political growth, who like additional facets of intrigue, romance, and social inspection added into the mix, will find *Replaced Parts* an intriguing story. It's powered by a strong first-person adventure that keeps readers on edge and guessing as Sierra evolves, both in her psychological development and by recognizing the ultimate purpose and impact of her efforts to save her father."

D. DONOVAN, SENIOR REVIEWER, Midwest Book Review

"With just the right mixture of science fiction and action/adventure, I love the unexpected twists and mysteries that the characters encounter. The way that the multiple dystopian worlds come together on their adventures is unpredictable, and it is all wrapped up with an unforeseen yet satisfying conclusion."

Reviewed By Amy Powers for Readers' Favorite

"The best part of the book is the romance between Austria and Josh, and the ending. And the parts having to do with the lives of the street kids."

Carol Cartaino, former Editor-in-Chief, Writer's Digest Books

"I'm always happy when Irish folklore is added to a story, we don't see enough of the Irish myths and legends in books. I thought Molly and Orla were interesting and unique characters and enjoyed getting to know them and the rest of the cast. I was invested in the plot and thought it was a good way of a potential series."

Kathryn M, NetGalley Reviewer

ALSO BY STEPHANIE HANSEN

Altered Helix

Stranded Coil

Paralleled Bond

Replaced Parts

Omitted Pieces

Ghostly Howls

SUGGESTED READING ORDER

Altered Helix (Altered Helix 1)

Stranded Coil (Altered Helix 2)

Paralleled Bond (Altered Helix 3)

Replaced Parts (Transformed Nexus 1)

Omitted Pieces (Transformed Nexus 2)

Armored Hours (Reincarnation Spells 1)

Ghostly Howls (Ghostly 1)

Ghostly Returns (Ghostly 2) – not yet released

Guarded Time (Reincarnation Spells 2) - not yet released

ARMORED HOURS

Stephanie Hansen

HYPOTHESIS
productions

Copyright © 2024 by Stephanie Hansen

All rights reserved. Published by Hypothesis Productions.

HYPOTHESIS
productions

The publisher doesn't have control over & doesn't assume any responsibility for author or third-party websites or their content.

No part of this publication may be reproduced, stored in a retrieval system, or transmitted in any form by any means, electronic, mechanical, photocopying, recording, or otherwise, without written permission of the publisher.

This book is a work of fiction. Names, characters, and incidents are either the product of the author's imagination or are used fictitiously, and any resemblance to actual persons, living or dead, or events is entirely coincidental.

ISBN 978-1-7350423-6-7

1 2 3 4 5 6 7 8 9 10

Printed in the U.S.A. First printing, 2024

The text type was set in Castellar, Harlow, and Times New Roman. Cover design by Fay Lane. Interior artwork by Jenna Hansen and @flandivel. Editing by Tru Story and Readers Together.

For those fighting bigotry and hate—you are loved, you are seen.

ARMORED HOURS

Stephanie Hansen

PROLOGUE – ALEXANDER

MISSING

On the evening of January 25, 1921, Claudia Walker (r.)–the daughter of the late Mr. Sebastian Walker and his widow, Marie Edwards Walker–went missing along with three friends and the rest of the passengers and crew aboard the S.S. Hewitt. A search team is being organized, and the family is paying for travel. If you are interested in volunteering, please meet tomorrow, Friday the twenty-ninth at 9 a.m., at The Crestwood Shops located at 55th and Crestwood.

–FROM THE CLASSIFIEDS PAGE OF THE *KANSAS CITY TIMES*, THURSDAY, JANUARY 28, 1921

The sun bounced off the Fords, Chryslers, and even the Renaults parked in diagonal spaces at the Crestwood Shops. Windows larger than I'd ever seen were surrounded by the most elaborately carved wooden trim. Despite this display of extravagance, the building was simply made of plain brick and mortar. One might think they would have shipped marble in for their desired center. The swankiest players in the city gathered in an attempt to bring their darling home. Only I knew Claudia was no darling, and she'd despise such attention. But who could really blame them? Nothing had ever drawn me in like her stunning figure, luscious dark hair, and mischievous smile.

It was cold as the dickens as I approached the shop. Pulling up the collar on my coat, I took a deep breath before I entered. People stood in every pocket of space available. Finery was displayed under glass counters. A man in a three-piece suit with wide lapels and high rise cuffed trousers more expensive than I'd ever own was leaning over the counter, speaking closely with a woman while smoking a cigarette. She laughed at something he said.

The more I hung around these people, the more I saw why Claudia disliked many of them. Miniature chandeliers dangled from the ceiling, providing a dim glow. In a corner, another man was holding a map of ship routes, trying to figure out where Claudia could have disappeared. The woman next to him had taken his hat and perched it jauntily upon her head. She looked as if she'd stolen his cookie, pleased as punch. The cluster of diamonds at her neck sparkled as she moved. It was difficult to think that any of them were taking this seriously. I gritted my teeth.

I also noticed that not a one of them uttered a single word about Claudia's closest friends who were also missing. Bubbly Kiersten, wickedly smart Lina, and artistic Florian would get no attention here because, like me, they were from the working class. Her mother, Marie, never approved of Claudia and I's relationship. There would be no permission granted when I, Alexander, asked for Claudia's hand in marriage. Not that she'd ever marry. She was too independent for that.

I think her penchant for rebelling is what's truly behind this disappearance. Too many husbands upset with her doling out birth control while helping me profit during the prohibition. Clinics all over the country had been raided. I knew gathering the next shipment in hopes of securing smuggled birth control would be risky.

Kiersten was the one to get word of the goods that could be on the steamship they were last seen on. She'd worked at one restaurant after another, which led her to connect

Claudia and me to every speakeasy contact she had. Kiersten was famous for her bangle bracelets. Depending on which one she wore, customers were privy to whether an undercover police officer was among them or not.

Most patrons also knew about the demise of Kiersten's mother at an early age. After one Southside Cocktail, it wasn't uncommon for Kiersten to speak about how witnessing almost a dozen births and just as many miscarriages slowly withered her mom away into oblivion. She had a way with storytelling that often won people over. It had been upon her instigation the girls decided to use a partial rum-runner to also move feminist contraband.

Lina was the one to cite laws of different jurisdictions, giving the group the best locations for our activities. She also mapped out the most efficient rail navigation to take the goods from the port. Plus, Lina was ever vigilant of the weather and what was a necessity to pack. Being multilingual, she'd been the one to communicate with our allies from other countries.

More loyal than I'd ever witnessed. I was glad she was with Claudia and Kiersten. Her analyzation skills are better than most in military intelligence, so hopefully she'll be able to lead them to safety. It was even rumored that during a trip to St. Louis, Lina befriended a woman named Bessie Coleman, who knew how to fly. She seemed to have an inclination to run in brilliant groups of resistance and drive despite the odds.

Last but certainly not least, Florian was the glue that kept them all together. I can picture her clasping her hands and then opening them in order to bring the entire group into a hug. Of course, then there would be a flurry about as she fixed hair and applied makeup on everyone. Always an air of mystery about her, she drew in many of our clients. Simply walking into a room, heads turned her way. But beauty is a precarious kind of power. It balances on a tightrope; one side, a netted catch of spectacular victory and the other a cement landing of doom. It's hard to tell whether her presence with them would solicit a bribe to freedom or have them all walking the plank. But I knew there was no way they'd go on this trip without Florian.

Just then, Marie Edwards Walker stepped onto a soapbox to address the crowd, and my attention moved from my own thoughts to the present moment. A fur around her shoulders and a cloche hat atop her head, she didn't need a microphone for everyone to hear her in the shop. Even her Shalimar perfume reached me.

"Attention, attention. Thank you all for coming here to support me in my search for my missing daughter, Claudia."

Oohs and ahhs filled the area with the mention of their darling. It packed me with anger, their fake devotion. But their pockets were loaded, and that's why I'd come here; to get money so I could find and save the love of my life.

There's one thing I do know for sure, they're not just missing but they're also in trouble. Ships don't just go missing. Their size alone makes that quite a feat. Even a wreck, though I truly hoped that was not the case, would leave a considerable amount of material behind. They're not just in trouble, but in danger.

My heart raced and the hairs on my neck stood up as I spun around in search of the source of my physical discomfort. There he was, Kris Mardell, smugness plastered across his lips and an evil look radiating from his now hooded eyes. A man who had ruined countless lives through his corruptness.

As I trembled with fear, Kris slowly withdrew a red silk tie from his pocket. It was none other than the one Claudia had bought me. I hadn't been able to hold onto it long before she stole it from me to wear all the time. In fact, her mother mentioned that she'd been wearing it when she left. Sweat beading down my forehead, I lunged for him with remarkable speed, despite the icy glares from the crowd. I would not let him take away yet another piece of my life.

Armored Hours

CHAPTER ONE – CLAUDIA

THE NICHOLS FAMILY
EXTENDS AN INVITATION FOR YOU TO ATTEND
A BALL IN HONOR OF THE BUILDER
PAUL M. FOGEL
ON THE EVENING OF SATURDAY
THE NINETEENTH OF JUNE THE YEAR 1920
AT EIGHT O'CLOCK AT PLA-MOR BALLROOM
NO. 3142 MAIN STREET
IN THE CITY OF KANSAS

FORMAL DRESS REQUIRED

"And this is the largest swimming pool west of the Mississippi River," Paul M. Fogel told Marie Edwards Walker and her daughter, Claudia, as he gestured to the water. To Claudia, it felt more like a bath house being inside. She'd snuck into Chicago's Douglass Park Pool with friends at night before. Nothing could counter the glee of swimming under the moonlight.

Of course, Marie had requested the tour so her daughter could spend more time with one of the most eligible bachelors in Kansas City. At first, dazzled by the multi-colored electric lighting of the ballroom, Claudia was now growing tired. To occupy her time, she began looking for an escape from her mother's persistent matchmaking attempts of courtship. They moved to the lower floor.

"We have all sorts of entertainment, including a bowling alley," Paul continued while winking at Claudia, as if he could read that she was growing tiresome. The sounds of bowling balls crashing into pins and the pocketing of balls at the billiards tables soothed Claudia, nonetheless. It felt not as pretentious and more like where she belonged. Plus, the sounds drowned out her tinnitus. When she'd survived meningitis at the age of ten, it had left her with unilateral deafness, resulting in a constant ringing in her head.

As Paul took Marie's arm to discuss the building process in more detail, Claudia made her extrication. While a couple of years younger, Paul was closer to Marie's age than Claudia's anyway. Perhaps her widowed mother could finally move on. A storage room devoid of most of the tables and chairs, which were now placed on the sides of the ballroom, had a faint glow to it.

She could just make out Kiersten's jubilant voice floating from the door as she approached. The smell of Florian's cigarette smacked Claudia in the face and she smiled. Lina called a raise at a makeshift poker table, much to the other players' chagrin. Claudia breathed in the life of the room. It was free of her mother's torturous societal charade.

Florian sat proudly, wearing the little black dress she had fashioned herself, inspired by Coco Chanel's style, which hadn't even made its way to Kansas City yet. Kiersten had everyone in stitches from one of her legendary jokes. Lina's sharp eyes calculated as she studied her poker opponents around the table.

"Look what the cat dragged in," Kiersten announced upon discovering Claudia's entrance.

"Trust me, I would have preferred to be here much earlier," Claudia responded with a sly smirk.

"Would you like a Mary Pickford?" Florian asked, lifting her own cocktail.

"That would be splendid," Claudia responded with an appreciative smile.

"I'll get it." The attractive businessman who had folded his hand early rose to go to the bar. He was lanky with short, dirty blond hair. He appeared to be close to eighteen, just like Claudia. Younger than the other men in the room.

An unapproachable group, those within the storage room were tight knit and required an invitation to join. Not a fancy one like Claudia's mother's friends approved of, but more of a word-of-mouth kind. Claudia had been shocked to receive hers but had been told her public speaking ability was admired. She had a way, she guessed, to rally in the troops to fight for a righteous cause.

From there, they'd grown. Off to the side, at another table, were papers haphazardly strewn about instead of cards. Claudia headed in that direction as her friends finished their game of skill. Frank, a man in his twenties, was holding a paper up and reading it intently. He had a curiosity about him that forever fascinated Claudia.

"What news do we have today?" Claudia asked him.

"You know how Mayor Cowgill has always been empathetic to citizens?" Frank asked her without looking away from his paper.

"Yeah?" She wasn't sure where Frank was going with this.

"He helped keep this city alive during the flu pandemic," Frank said while raising his eyebrows.

Claudia peered at the paper Frank was holding. It had a photo of a prescription pad.

"Yes, and now…he's continuing to help by passing the local medicinal purposes law," Frank added.

"He did?"

"Now, with a doctor's note, Kansas Citians will be able to procure alcohol at any permitted drug store. Luckily, we don't need such a document here." Frank winked.

"Let me see that," Kiersten said, reaching over Claudia's shoulder. She'd come up from behind and draped herself on her friend as Frank spoke. He reluctantly handed her the paper.

Claudia smiled at Kiersten and then read alongside her. "Too bad a prescription pad like that with birth control written on it instead of liquor would be seen as obscene!"

"Speaking of"–Kiersten turned Claudia around by her shoulders and hooked an arm in hers–"the girls need to discuss a new development." She handed the paper back to Frank before they walked to the poker table.

Florian was dealing another hand in which she included Claudia this time. Her long fingers delicately flicked card after card to the desired person. Even in poker, she had a certain style about her that Claudia envied.

"We've heard from our friends in Tennessee," Lina said after Kiersten nodded, giving her the go ahead. Most of the men in the room had moved to gather at the table of papers to discuss the possibilities with the new law in place.

"Oh?" Claudia watched Lina ponder before answering. Her friend was so intelligent that local businessmen often consulted with her over decisions, but they never formally gave her a seat at the meetings, which was a travesty for sure. How much they could gain if only women were allowed to join.

"The state's primed for ratification," Lina finally answered. "Women all over America might be able to vote on November 2nd!"

"Yeah, there's going to be a rally in Nashville!" Kiersten couldn't hold back her excitement. To her, travel was freedom. It was something her mother had never been able to do and, therefore, Kiersten felt the need to fill that void. To go to all of the places her mother never could and leave a mark there. It was as if she believed leaving those imprints for her mother all over the world, that her spirit would live on forever and everywhere.

"The Nashville ladies do have some of the most rebellious fashion," Florian added.

"How will we get there?" Claudia asked, leaning forward intently. She shoved her quandaries down and chose to participate in her friends' excitement rather than bring up negativity. The thought of how even with ratification, not all women would have the right to vote could be tackled another time.

"First, Capt. John S. Campbell has agreed to get us to St. Louis and, then, we'll hop on the Dixie Flyer." Lina always coordinated their travel navigation.

"Here you go," the handsome young man who had offered to get Claudia's drink had returned.

"Why thank you, good sir," Claudia said with a smile; a rose color rushing to her cheeks. She reached for the drink and nodded in appreciation.

"Alexander"–he had a sheepish grin on his face–"but you can call me Alex."

"Thank you, Alex. I'm Claudia." She extended her hand, and he took it; planting a kiss on top of it. Claudia's heart beat wildly when he looked back up into her eyes.

"What's this about Captain Campbell?" Alexander asked them. "Will you be onboard a steamboat in the near future?"

"That's none of your business," Kiersten snapped. Then, with her thumb, she pointed at the men behind her. "Shouldn't you be over there?"

"What they're discussing isn't of any interest to me." He shrugged and then looked at Claudia. "I'm much more interested in what's over here."

"And why aren't you interested in what's over there?" Lina asked, raising an eyebrow while also lifting her cards to see what hand she was dealt.

"Because, there's no money in it." Alexander huffed. "No one's going to want to talk to their doctor about how much they need alcohol."

"How uncouth of you!" Florian rolled her eyes.

All of the young ladies had peeked at their cards and were going around the table; each making their own move.

"It's not uncouth of me! I have a sick ma and younger sibling at home. I have to consider in my decision making."

"You're taking care of them?" Lina asked.

"How are we supposed to believe this guy? We just met him." Kiersten gestured in Alexander's direction.

"I believe him," Claudia responded.

"I have a picture of them in my pocket right here." He reached into his chest coat pocket. Claudia's eyes were locked on the item that looked like a pocket watch as he pulled it out. Instead of being thick and able to open, the circular shape (more oval than circle) was metal on one side, but held a picture covered in glass on the other side. Instead of the hands of a clock, she saw two figures.

"What's that?" Claudia asked Alex, reaching for the item.

"It's a locket, and this is a picture of my ma and little brother." He held it closer for her to be able to see.

Florian examined the young man skeptically, not expecting such open responses. His light brown hair was slicked back and his eyes flicked between Lina and Claudia. "So, if you're not lying and you need money, what are you doing over here?" Florian asked.

"A contact of mine says we can get good whiskey not yet confiscated from Tennessee, so when I overheard your conversation, I thought perhaps we could work together."

"You want to work with us?" Lina held a dubious look upon her face.

"Well, you've got good transportation planned if you really are traveling with Captain Campbell. Sounds like you're taking the train after St. Louis. Why wouldn't I want to work with you?"

Lina's jaw dropped slightly at his daring attitude, and Claudia stepped in for her.

"What are your views on women's rights?" she asked cautiously.

His lips thinned as he considered her question, then he exhaled heavily while shaking his head slowly. "I think women should have all the rights. Do you know what I would give if Ma could have had more control of the finances before my pa passed?" He paused, and the group remained silent, reflecting on his heartfelt response.

Finally, Lina nodded in approval and spoke up again. "He can help lift our bags," she said simply, and there was a moment of understanding among them all that this enigma of a man must have tentatively earned their trust.

Florian clasped her hands together joyfully and exclaimed, "You have to let me style you!"

Claudia smiled and interrupted calmly, "I raise." She rubbed her palm on her thigh to soothe an itch, prompting Alex to comment.

"You know, some say itchy palms are a sign that one is about to come into money," Alex told Claudia, leaning into her, and they both smiled, as if telling an inside secret the two had held for years.

CHAPTER TWO – ALEXANDER

C~

CHAMBERLAIN SENT A WARNING

THERE'S TO BE A RAID

TELL KIERSTEN

LINA SHOULD MEET MS. CHAMBERLAIN

AND SHE HAS GARMENTS FOR FLORIAN

~A

"Move these to the attic." Kiersten pointed to a few cases of full bottles. "There's a hidden compartment at the end. I'll show you how to access it."

My crew and I followed her, with Claudia in tow. I had hoped the weather would be a little cooler than normal Kansas City summer temperatures for this undertaking. I removed my tweed vest and hung it on a barstool. Then, I wiped sweat off my brow with my flat cap. As I rolled up my sleeves, Claudia opened her feather fan to cool me. I smiled at her, even though the fan had little effect.

Unlike the Chamberlain mansion, this establishment did not have air conditioning. To be fair, few places did. Anna Chamberlain had a way of getting what she wanted. That's what happens when your business attracts rich and powerful people. Luckily, the entry to the attic was a rectangle in the ceiling, allowing for a slanted staircase when lowered instead of a ladder. It made moving Kiersten's booze much easier. But it also made me worry, as it would surely be seen during a raid.

"Here, let me take one," Claudia said to James as he set down the two cases he'd been carrying to adjust for the climb. James was probably the hardest worker in my crew.

"I can just make a second trip. It's no problem."

"Oh, don't be silly. You think I haven't transported one of these before for my best friend?" Claudia teased.

With that, James raised his eyebrows. Claudia deftly lifted the case, and he huffed out in surprise.

The attic smelled of dust, dirt, and old books. Primarily filled with boxes, there was a nook off to the right with the only window in the space. A small table with a couple of chairs was tucked under the natural light. Maps, notes, and teacups covered the table. This must be a spot the girls meet to discuss plans. Away from the patrons, where not a peep would be heard, and with a spectacular view of the heart of our city.

Kiersten walked to the end of the attic and knelt down next to the two feet base boards I hadn't noticed before. Barely visible to the naked eye, she grabbed hold of a small piece of ribbon and then proceeded to pull it until the board flopped open. Once set aside, I saw that plenty of cases could be hidden in this compartment.

"Don't worry, there aren't any hidden bodies," Kiersten joked.

After laughing, James and Thomas quickly pushed a couple of cases in far enough, and I couldn't help but think that the space had to be at least four feet deep. A body really could be hidden in there! Friendly Thomas was always ready for a laugh, but it was nice to see James join in too. We had the first round in place in no time and went for the next.

It was good to see the two groups working together in mutual respect. Watching Claudia ascend the ladder wasn't half bad either. The way her legs moved as she walked showed her grace but also her strength. The hem of her day dress fell just below her knees. The way the drop waist moved with her hips distracted me enough that I ran into a table.

My eyes were drawn to her, no matter how hard I tried to look away. Her arms were also bare, but none of her features could hold a candle to her beautiful face. Her smile knocked the wind out of me. She was watching Kiersten return the board as we'd been able to fit all of the cases in the hidden compartment, and I was reminded again of how vulnerable this hiding spot was. As gently as I could, I placed my hand on Claudia's elbow.

"We should move some of the boxes in front of the base boards just in case," I whispered.

Claudia looked at me, perplexed.

"Sorry, didn't mean to overstep." I held up my hands.

"You're on the wrong side," Kiersten said. "Try whispering in her other ear." She winked at me.

Claudia looked back behind us, offering me her other ear and in a regular voice instead of whispering, I told her about the boxes this time.

Claudia looked back and eyed the ribbon Kiersten kept hold of while replacing the board. Her forehead scrunched a little in between her brows. "Yeah, that's not a bad idea."

James and Thomas were right on it. My anxiety greatly decreased once they moved the first stack closer to the wall. I moved the next stack and then took a seat at the table by the window to gather myself.

"May I?" Claudia asked, referring to if she could take the other chair even though these belonged more to her than me.

I gestured for her to go ahead, and she silently sat down. Next, out of the corner of my eye, I could see she was sneaking glances at me too. She smiled as our gazes connected. It sent an intoxicating shiver up my spine.

"Thank you for helping us," she said on an exhale.

"Kiersten's a good customer," I responded, leaning back to get more comfortable. "If you ever need anything, just let me know."

She smirked. "Kiersten's the best." Claudia rubbed dust from the candlestick on the table. "I appreciate your offer."

"But...?" I replied. "There's often a 'but' after that statement."

"We manage just fine on our own most of the time."

"Yes, you all seem very competent, but everyone needs a little help sometimes."

"Well, then, how about if YOU ever need anything, just let US know," she countered.

"Agreed." I stuck out my hand out of habit and, when she grabbed it with her own, a jolt of electricity shot up my arm and my heart skipped a beat. I cleared my throat.

"Come on," Kiersten said. "Customers should be arriving any minute now."

"You've prepared them for the raid?" I asked.

"Florian made a few house calls, and Kiersten has her own way of letting customers know," Claudia interjected.

"Of course." Kiersten held up her arm and rattled her bangle bracelets. "I have a new color!"

"Cat's out of the bag now!" Claudia hugged Kiersten from the side.

"What cat? New color?" Thomas asked, examining the bracelets to see what was so special.

"Blue means there's an undercover cop present. Green means we're free to do as we wish. And, now, red means there's going to be a raid!"

"That's brilliant," James exclaimed. They were all so close together and full of joy, as if they'd been lifelong friends. It made me happy to see James and Thomas cheerful, too, after everything we've been through.

As patrons filtered in, it was hard for me to imagine the impending racket that would be occurring soon. The air was merry, the area softly lit, and conversational laughter bounced all around. This was the side of what I did that most people never thought about.

Sure, alcohol has its issues, but the way it brings people together is surreal. Even though there would only be tea and coffee on this day, it didn't seem to matter much. Everyone was fine just enjoying each other's company.

Kiersten ran things without a hitch, brewing the most delectable non-alcoholic drinks of all time. Serving many tables as well as the bar without breaking a sweat. Claudia read a book while sipping tea at the bar. I wished I could sit next to her, but Thomas, James, and I needed to have eyes on the door.

Despite the calm start, the night wasn't completely devoid of drama before the raid. Thomas discovered a woman as she was entering, noting the unneeded cane she was using. Its handle could be removed in order to store alcohol in the base. This way, people could add liquor to a regular drink ordered from a restaurant.

We didn't need something so trivial to cause the shutdown of Kiersten's place of employment. James removed a man from the premises who tried to drop our code word at the bar. Tonight, we needed to appear like complete teetotalers. Had it just been a stool pigeon who informed the cops of this place, perhaps a couple bribes could get them to turn the other way. But I had a sneaking suspicion that what we had on our hands was someone singing like a canary. Nope, not a drop of hooch would be found here.

When the front door did finally slam open, anger immediately rose throughout my body. It was none other than Vernon Floyd, a man I had deemed my mortal foe. Parading around as a clean-cut police officer, he was actually one of my strongest rivals in the bootlegging business. The fact that he pushed out most of his competitors with hypocritical ticketing and arrests was only the tip of the iceberg. Unfortunately, it didn't surprise me that recently I'd heard talk about him and other "peacekeepers" uniting to add poison to bootlegged alcohol in order to deter customers from buying from anyone but him and his cronies. He was ruthless.

The doorknob slammed into the wall as he stepped through the doorway. "Stay where you are. We're searching the premises, including everyone inside," Vernon yelled.

Other cops stormed in past him. One went behind the bar, opening drawers and spilling their contents on the floor.

He smelled the coffee, then dumped it in the sink and repeated the process with the tea. Kiersten stared at him with a look that could only be described as violent.

Another cop walked to the tables. "Empty your pockets," he ordered the customers. "Do as you're told and things will go better for you."

The patrons looked annoyed with him, but put the contents of their pockets and purses in front of the cop as requested. The cop actually laughed at the small amount of cash one man had. He looked at the woman with him and said, "You should improve your taste in men."

I could tell she had to bite her tongue not to mouth off. She probably wanted to say how much more of a man hers was than this cop.

Vernon walked over to the shelves housing dishes and wickedly knocked one over, breaking everything it had been holding. There was no way any alcohol could have been hidden in there. He didn't need to cause such damage.

Kiersten could no longer hold back. "Are you going to pay for that?"

Vernon marched right over to her and pulled out his gun without hesitation.

"There's no need." Claudia softly put her hand on Vernon's forearm. Even though his uniform was long-sleeved and, therefore, she wasn't even really touching him, I felt a wave of jealousy wash over me.

James, Thomas, and I all stood up. "Is that how you treat a lady?" I asked.

"Well, well, there's got to be liquor here with this crew in attendance." Luckily, Vernon holstered his gun. "Place your belongings on the bar."

We did as we were told. I stepped between Claudia and Vernon to do so; with the largest smirk planted on my face. I was glad Anna had warned us of the raid so that I could be sure not to have my usual flask in my pocket. Not only did she help boost local women looking for independence, she had a soft spot in her heart for me, given my ma's condition. Vernon looked over our stuff, upset with finding nothing. He did, however, pick up my locket.

"It would be a shame for something to happen to this." He held it out in front of him; dangling it by the chain as if he were going to drop it and stomp it to smithereens. Things froze, and my breath caught as he threatened my dearest material possession.

"Hey, Lieutenant, there's something up here," one of the cops yelled out.

Relief washed over me as Vernon put the locket back on the bar, but my fear was overshadowed by the worry of them finding the attic. They opened the rectangle in the ceiling, revealing the slanted staircase. With every boot pound on the stairs, my heart hammered in my chest. Once they were all in the attic, I looked at Claudia, whose eyes were as big as saucers. "Keep cool," I said to her.

Claudia looked at Kiersten and made a couple of hand gestures that I didn't recognize. With hands facing toward the ground, her pinky and thumb out, she lowered them. Then, with flat hands, she held them out in front of her chest and lowered them toward the ground with her elbows tucked at her sides. She and Kiersten both took deep breaths. I'm not sure what form of communication they were using, but the silent reassurance was endearing.

Thomas walked around to the tables, instructing everyone to gather their things just in case we needed to make a quick getaway. James hung out at the bottom of the stairs, listening to what was happening above. With the first hint that they'd found the hidden liquor, he'd close the door and block it; locking them in the attic. I nodded to Kiersten for her to gather the money so Vernon couldn't steal it, claiming it as evidence.

Silence had fallen upon the once jovial group. Heels tapped the floor in a nervous bounce, almost making the crowd seem as one. The tension was a tangible thing. Footsteps could be heard above as the officers invaded our privacy. Moving over our heads in a back-and-forth pattern.

Thoughts danced around my brain. Were they looking in the boxes? Did we cover the baseboards entirely? What were they doing?! Finally, a boot appeared on the top step, and they made their way back downstairs.

"Nothing here," Vernon exclaimed, back to yelling. "Looks like someone tipped them off." He made eye contact directly with me.

Then he was next to Claudia again. "Your mom know you're here?"

"I'm an adult now," she barked.

"I recognized the handwriting on that table up there," Vernon continued. "You should really be careful with what you're doing. Could get in a lot of trouble."

"I can take care of myself."

Then, it was his turn to smirk at me. "Wouldn't want to have to arrest you. You're far too pretty for jail."

It took every ounce of my being not to deck him right then and there.

Chapter Three - Marie

Armored Hours

Let's start with the end, shall we? I'd say, "rip off the band-aid", but since the contraption was only invented recently, you may not be familiar with the saying. I, of course, am an anomaly, so the phrase is quite familiar. When Sebastian died, a part of me went with him.

It's strange. I thought memories would only flow to later bodies in reincarnation. For me, memories flow in both directions (future to past and past to future). I hold some from bodies that have yet to be as well as people from the past. In the beginning, my parents almost locked me up, fearing I was seeing things that weren't there.

I've learned to suppress these thoughts from other times now. And yet, with the knowledge comes responsibility that requires me to act upon them. I had tried to do so when the information surfaced of my beloved's upcoming passing. But I'd been unable to stop it. Perhaps some timelines just can't be altered. I do know that I will make them pay for what they've done, though. It's all their fault.

"Welcome, dear, please do have a seat," the woman in a colorful shawl, Nelly, gestures toward the round table at the center of the room with two cushioned chairs beside it. Here, she goes by the name Nelly, even though she's known as

Ellen in our societal circle. As Ellen, she's a successful dress manufacturer employing hundreds of local women. As Nelly, she's allowed to step away from her rigid professional environment to one more mystical.

Candles provide the only light, their fire flickering, as if dancing to a silent song. At the center of the table is a crystal ball. It sits atop a silver tripod base with ornately curled legs. There's also a glass jar for tips which Nelly eyes as she sits down, indicating that I should add to the pile now. Another thing the law has taken from us, she's not allowed to charge for readings outright (though Nelly's always donated her reading funds anyway, but still). She's only allowed to accept tips now. Looking at me, she holds her arms out and around the ball, close but leaving a bit of distance, as if an invisible force field surrounds it.

Future memories of my fingers brilliantly strumming piano keys allow me to have the capability to do so in this life. It's rather amazing to carry talents through the ages and be able to soak up skills across time. Making reincarnation fluid with immortality, I feel like a magical being. But, even those with powers experience struggles.

Thoughts flowing back and forth through time to multiple bodies can be disorienting. Was it the verbal poetry incanting reincarnation or the ability to travel to other worlds with a mere thought that brought me here? What the books don't warn you about is that soaking these spells into your bones causes it to pass on to your descendants. There are actually quite a few of us all around you.

One might see the distinction if they really tried. We don't fall easy prey to our counters like you do. They travel not out of survival or rescuing. They travel for control. Counters don't reincarnate solely to protect their loved ones, but have taken it a step further. They've made the leap to vengeance beyond reason, a devotion without limitation. You'd probably recognize our counters if you looked hard enough too. They're also milling about in your everyday life.

"I will see what I see and no more. What do you need to know most?" Nelly stares at me with a concentrated look. Her long, dark hair flows down under her silk headdress. She takes in a deep breath, and I do the same while contemplating exactly how to ask what I need to know.

Setting a plain, white collar that had been part of men's fashion in the 1600s on the table, I say, "I need to find two souls linked to this."

She picks it up and examines it, seeming to avail her mind, allowing all of its details to be absorbed. A lotus scent wafts out from her homemade candles. I'm not sure how she did it with what's available to her in this period, but the effect is magnificent.

Even further into the future, I have memories of studying meditation and psychology. Really thinking about it, I realize those practices stem from a past hundreds of years before now. At a moment of emergency, I invoked transmigration via hyper focused rumination.

You see, my sister, she was the one who always had the most wisdom and kindness. She had more than I could ever hope for, but it caused her to not allow injustice and to stand face to face with the enemy in moments of pure terror. We lost her too early, before she could watch her remaining children grow, but not before she could take a disastrous step for her love.

With her passing, her other half went mad. I could understand his undeniable rage. I've felt it myself. But I didn't act on it quite like he did. I vowed to keep her memory alive, her spirit going. He vowed to be sure all who could have stopped her demise from happening would suffer for eternity.

Across from me, Nelly closes her eyes, gathering an internal picture of the information being fed to her from the collar in her hands. A vibration radiates through the air, sending the candle flickers into a craze. A prickling sensation runs across my skin. In her brogue accent, she says, "Focus on the now."

Her hands shake ever so slightly as she places them on the ball, staring into it, full of concentration. I do my best to push out interrupting thoughts, to follow her instruction. Then, fuzzy images appear to me in my mind's eye. The taste of gin fills my mouth from nowhere.

Her sharp intake of air can be heard throughout the room. I too fill my lungs with oxygen. Dozens of thoughts abruptly drown my meditation, and I am no longer able to glimpse into whatever it is she's seeing.

With his passionate vengeance, my sister's lover has been more successful than I, for she lives longer each return, partly due to his actions. But something stunted his progress in the distant future and now he's done the unfathomable. Somehow, he's spawned back twice over. While the rest of us have one distinct past, he's caused his pathway to fork.

What his twin lifeline could mean for the universe is incomprehensible. That the same line can run parallel with itself is an abomination to our world. It will surely bring about its end. Right now, he's focused on this timeline and, so far, I've been able to keep my sister hidden. She's placed in the most unlikely of stations. I try to feel his presence to be sure he doesn't get too close, but it's been a struggle to even identify both versions of him. He's the worst counter of them all.

"One likes to appear as obedient, but he traipses through the shadows as disobedient as can be. The other doesn't hide his violations." Nelly's eyes remain glued to the crystal ball she holds. "The first was recently near your blood and the other soon will be."

Sebastian had been the one who noticed a heavy force around us. He'd investigated the best he could, using scientific and spiritual knowledge to decipher clues. I had warned him not to get too close, but he didn't listen. Some need to protect clouded his brain and now I've lost the armor of him completely; well, at least in this timeline.

It's odd knowing how he looks throughout all of our timelines. We always find one another; it was written in the stars, far beyond our control. I need to know more. What did Nelly mean by close to my blood before and soon? How close are they? She said she would only see what she sees and nothing more, but she's still transfixed by something. "Go on."

"The first one will try to use the law to capture her and the second will try to use her vulnerability." Nelly releases the ball and leans back into her chair.

In the past, my sister had been a spy for him. Traipsing in and out of enemy territory in order to bring him the vital information he needed. She was head over heels for him and naïve as can be. The tenacity to persevere naturally held as well as her intelligence. It's what's always attracted him to her. But there's also been an ulterior motive, even when he loved her with all that he had.

He just couldn't deny that part of himself. The ever incessant droning on of the marching to the beat of superior achievement. As if it's ingrained into his very DNA. The man never waivers, never runs short of drive. Perhaps that's why they always find one another. So, not only have I had to keep an eye on him. I've had to keep her preoccupied too.

In this life, my sister is a well-established entrepreneur in the great town of Kansas City. Her determination might even outstand his. Having to deal with many awful situations, she's proven rather resourceful. While there's an age gap between us in this life, it didn't stop my Sebastian from helping her find the best radios for her establishment.

He also helped my sister plan a concert at the mansion. Though she'd been successful for years, prohibition greatly decreased the ability for her to earn the same profit. The fine wine at her resort had been an absolute hit, but those days were becoming more and more difficult. Her business attracted rich and powerful men from all over, so perhaps the drop in success would help me hide her from him, her soulmate throughout time.

I express my gratitude to Nelly. She nods, but seems to be in a daze of sorts. As we stand, she falters and catches herself. When her hand hits the table, it also makes contact with the collar. "Special care needs to be taken when handling <u>shiny</u> weapons. No, I meant shiny armor."

"Are you okay? What are you talking about?" I put my hands on her shoulders to be sure she's steady. Then, I grab the collar from her hand, and she breathes in, as if she'd been holding her breath for minutes.

She smiles at me and seems to be sturdy again. "Oh, that was different. The object seemed to speak to me without the help of the crystal ball. It even spoke through me."

"What do you think it meant?"

She ponders over it for a bit and then says, "Perhaps moonshine, yes, it must have meant moonshine."

The taste of gin fills my mouth again as I depart. That must be the clue I need to follow.

Sebastian always had an investigative personality about him, which also led to him continuously seeking to improve things. He would know exactly what to do with this clue.

Even thinking about him now, tears well up. I miss him so much; the feeling of loss is all that remains. He's the complete opposite of the counter who is ever so calculating; contemplating things no one else sees and making the chess moves no one expects. While trying to find my sister, he took Sebastian, my soulmate. In this lifetime, my sister's name is Anna Chamberlain, and I will never let him, either of his twin lines, near her again. Even if it indicates having to do something I never thought I would do. What this will mean to our paths, I cannot know. As the reincarnation passed, so did more responsibility. With this new change, many events might be transformed. For the better or worse, only destiny can decide.

CHAPTER FOUR – CLAUDIA

WELCOME TO THE CHAMBERLAIN RESORT

WOMEN WILL BE TREATED WITH RESPECT HERE
ANYONE NOT FOLLOWING THIS RULE WILL BE REMOVED
PLEASE ENJOY YOUR STAY AND HAVE A GOOD TIME
PLENTY OF THE BEST WINES AND CIGARS ARE AVAILABLE

~ ANNA CHAMBERLAIN

As Claudia and her friends followed Alex's crew through the ornate entrance of the Chamberlain Mansion, they were immediately struck by the grandeur of their surroundings. The walls were adorned with intricate carvings and mirrors of French plate glass, while the ceiling displayed a breathtaking gilded metal fresco that seemed to come alive in the flickering candlelight. Even the floor was a sight to behold, with delicate tile work that shimmered underfoot.

Despite its opulence, the mansion held a dark secret—it was a bordello. However, as Claudia and her friends looked around, they couldn't help but be amazed at how it appeared unlike anything they'd expected in a brothel. Something dank as a basement, with leering men all around, would have been closer to what they had envisioned. The lavish furnishings and tasteful decor were more fitting for a high-end manor than a place of what some might refer to as 'ill repute.' And to their surprise, they recognized some of the patrons from Claudia's mother's elegant society affairs.

The women in attendance were dressed in clothing that exuded wealth and luxury, each article worth more than Kiersten's entire monthly income. Claudia knew because she helped Kiersten keep the books from time to time. It was a stark contrast to the common perception of brothels, and Claudia couldn't help but wonder about the stories behind these wealthy men's presence at such a place. They moved to a private dining room next.

"Please, do have a seat." Anna gestured gracefully towards the elegant dining table. Her hair was styled in a precise center part, with sleek curls pinned up in an immaculate fashion. She exuded professionalism, wearing a tailored dress that could almost pass for a partial suit. The cuffs were adorned with four gleaming buttons, indicating the garment's high quality. Claudia couldn't help but be reminded of some of the pieces her mother had purchased from the renowned designer Ellen Donnelly Reed. Could it be possible that Anna and her mother had crossed paths before? Despite their age difference, there were certain similarities between the two that Claudia couldn't ignore.

As they all settled into their seats, Alex spoke up, "We just wanted to thank you again for giving us the heads-up last week, Anna."

Kiersten chimed in, "Seriously, we wouldn't have known what to do without your warning. We'd probably be sitting in jail right now."

Anna humbly waved away their gratitude. While she appreciated their thanks, she didn't want these kids to feel indebted in any way. Too often in her youth, people had expected something in return when they offered their help. The thought of a former colleague in a superior position to her own leaning in and whispering sexual innuendos sent a shudder through her.

Florian raised her glass of wine and examined it curiously. "What is this?" she asked with genuine interest. She swirled the liquid under her nose, inhaling deeply to take in its complex aroma. It was clear with a golden tint.

"That, my dear, is the infamous White Pearl from Stone Hill Winery," Anna replied, pride filling her at her investment in the prize-winning product. "And they have a wonderful handler." Anna winked at Alex.

Frank leaned in closer, his curiosity getting the better of him. "Is that the winery in Hermann?"

Lina chimed in eagerly, "They're known for making their own barrels from the nearby forest, right?"

"Well, aren't you the smart one?" Anna's smile widened as she looked at Lina. It was her mission in life to give women more options. She could only imagine what achievements Lina could experience if the world gave women the equal footing as men.

"How can you afford all of this?" Lina gestured around them, taking in the intricate decorations, expensive furniture, and fancy wine.

Anna's smirk returned as she casually replied, "I charge more than my competitors."

James raised an eyebrow in disbelief. "Why would anyone want to pay more?"

"For better quality, of course," Anna responded. "That… as well as burlesque and gambling." She winked.

Claudia couldn't help but recall the high society individuals she'd seen upon their entry. She looked up at the beautiful chandelier that hung from the ornate ceiling, casting a warm glow over the room.

"But do you pay your employees better too?" Kiersten asked with a bit of skepticism. She was accustomed to women being treated poorly and couldn't help herself from asking.

"That is an important question indeed." Anna smiled at the group, her gaze lingering on each person with genuine care. Having lost two pregnancies, one in a tragic carriage accident, it felt nice to be able to bestow wisdom and care to younger generations. "I protect my employees, do my best to ensure they earn a livable wage, and provide them with tools to grow. I see them as kindred spirits more than just employees."

"Huh, you've made this place feel exclusive. I can see why it would draw in more money than your competitors."

Lina, admiration evident in her voice, seemed proud of the successful Kansas City businesswoman.

Thomas grinned mischievously and added, "Nice enough to be a resort, if you ask me." His eyes sparkled with excitement at the thought of all the luxurious amenities Ms. Chamberlain had managed to incorporate into her establishment.

With a gentle creak, the old oak door swung open and in walked a stunning young woman, her arms overflowing with an array of vibrant garments. Her hair cascaded down her back in waves of golden honey, catching the light from the chandelier. "Florian, I thought you might be interested to see these." Anna stood from her seat at the long wooden table, smiling warmly at the woman and reaching out to take the top garment from her.

As Florian clapped her hands excitedly and rose from her chair, Claudia couldn't help but feel joy at seeing her friend's unbridled delight. As Anna approached, Florian's eyes were fixed on the garment in her hands, unable to tear them away from its beauty. With a nod of permission from Anna, Florian clasped her hands together in front of her and silently asked if she could touch the dress. Eyes twinkling indulgently, Anna extended it towards her for closer inspection. It was like a piece of art hanging on display, begging to be admired and appreciated. With bated breath,

Florian reached out and ran her fingers over the fabric, reveling in its softness and intricate details.

"The neckline is exquisite! The slanted angle is perfectly flattering," she gushed. Her eyes widened as she felt the durability of the material. "And look at how the waist cinches in just the right places!"

Anna nodded knowingly, a satisfied smile on her face. "Yes, this dress is designed to make every woman feel stunning. From delicate creatures like yourself to curvy beauties like me." A spark of pride glimmered in her eyes as she saw the joy on Florian's face at the custom creation.

Lina and Kiersten had now joined them, each holding up a garment in their hands. Kiersten marveled in shock at the toughness of the material. "This could even withstand the duties at my job," she exclaimed.

"The shoulder work is absolutely amazing," Lina added, her eyes gleaming with admiration. She carefully examined the sophisticated details, a testament to the skilled craftsmanship of the designer. "It exudes professionalism and class; fashion and durability all in one."

"The woman who runs the company also looks out for her employees," Anna added. "She's constantly working to provide comprehensive benefits like life insurance, medical support, pensions, a cafeteria, and education opportunities."

Lina's eyes widened in disbelief. "Did you just say a woman runs that place too?!"

Anna nodded proudly. "Yes! And she's an extraordinary leader."

As they continued to browse through the outfits, Claudia placed a grateful hand on Alex's arm and whispered, "Thank you. Actually, I have a gift for you." She pulled out a small box from her purse.

Alex opened it and pulled out a sophisticated tie. He flashed her a warm smile and raised his glass in a toast. Claudia clinked her glass with his and they both took a sip, savoring the moment of celebration together. The smooth wine danced across their taste buds, filling them with joy and gratitude. For the first time, Claudia actually considered letting a man into her heart.

Their moment of elation was abruptly shattered by a piercing, guttural scream that echoed from beyond the neighboring wall. Panic gripped their hearts as they braced themselves for whatever horror lurked on the other side. No one noticed that, while everyone's heads turned toward the sound, Claudia's was turned in the opposite direction briefly before she corrected herself after noticing where everyone else was looking. Unilateral deafness caused her not to be able to tell the direction of sound.

Anna burst through the doors of the dining room and into the dark hallway, her eyes blazing with fury. She was met with a disturbing scene—a man gripping a woman's hair, forcing her to kneel before him as she whimpered in pain. With a fierce shout, Anna demanded that he release her from his grasp.

As Claudia and Alex quickly followed her, they were aghast by the scene before them. The woman held her head as she grimaced in pain. Alex recognized the man mistreating the woman as Kris Mardell, another one of his fiercest bootlegging competitors. Kris sneered at them; his face contorted with anger.

"She's trying to gouge me with more than quadruple the price I pay down the street!" Kris spat out.

Anna's hand trembled with rage as she took a step closer, determined to protect the woman she considered a kindred spirit. "Perhaps you should stick to that territory and never set foot in ours again if our prices are too high for you," she retorted fiercely.

But just as tensions were rising to dangerous levels, a flash of metal caught their attention. A knife had been hurled across the hallway, narrowly missing Kris's head and embedding itself in the wooden column beside him. The threat was clear—he was not welcome here.

"The next one's in your eye if you don't let go of her right now," Kiersten, who had also rushed to the hallway, seethed with venom. She held another knife by the blade, tapping it on the side of her head, never taking her eyes off of Kris.

He reluctantly let go of the woman and held his shaking hands up. Then, he jeered at Alex. "Now I see where you got your overpriced booze." He lifted his chin in Alex's direction.

"It's not overpriced when it's the best in town." Alex smirked. Thomas, Frank, and James walked around their group to stand next to Kris. The tension in the air was thick as molasses.

"You better pay this fine young lady the money you owe her," Thomas barked. "Shoot, she deserves triple what she's charging for putting up with you."

Lina and Florian stood by, their faces twisted into expressions of disgust and contempt. "I believe many of your clients are our friends," Lina said. "It would be a shame if we had to tell them about your horrid behavior tonight."

"Yeah," Florian added with a malicious grin. "It would be a travesty; might even put you out of business."

Eyes hardened in anger, Frank and James stared at Kris while he paid what was due and then they inched closer to him, guiding him firmly out of the establishment.

While he retreated, he shouted back at Anna, "Don't think you're immune! I know you have connections with the Chief of police, but I have friends in the highest levels of government. And trust me, they're already talking about doubling the sin tax."

As soon as Kris disappeared from their view, Anna's body gave way and she collapsed to the floor next to the woman. Her breaths came in heaving gasps, her body overcome with exhaustion. "Dear, the doctor will be available soon," Anna reassured the girl, her voice soft and gentle. "Let him take a look at you and take the rest of the night off."

The woman protested weakly, "But I need the money…"

Anna placed a comforting hand on her shoulder. "Just keep the fifty percent that you usually give me. You've more than earned it."

Thomas's eyes widened in surprise and he glanced over at Alex. As Anna guided the woman up and out of the hallway, supporting her weight and steadying her frightened form, Thomas leaned in towards Alex and whispered, "I've never heard of such a generous cut. Rumor has it most places don't even let employees keep twenty-five percent, let alone fifty."

Lipreading this conversation and witnessing what had just transpired, Claudia's admiration for Anna only grew stronger. She silently vowed to work with Lina to ensure that Anna's taxes wouldn't increase. In that moment, Claudia saw Anna not just as a boss but as a kindhearted protector and advocate for those in need.

CHAPTER FIVE – ALEXANDER

ON BOARD THE MISSOURI
DINNER
TUNA FISH CANAPE
BAKED BARRACUDA, FINE HERBS
CAULIFLOWER IN CREAM
NEAPOLITAN ICE CREAM

The atmosphere in the forward lounge of THE MISSOURI steamboat was electric with celebration, but Claudia's demeanor betrayed a sense of unease. Her eyes darted around the room, scanning those nearby as if she were a seasoned detective on the trail of a dangerous suspect.

The reason for her worry became increasingly clear as I took in my surroundings. The whitewashed walls exuded a somberness that seemed to weigh heavily on us all. The harsh glow of incandescent light from above cast deep shadows into every corner, providing perfect hiding for anyone seeking to remain unseen. Even the dizzying patterns of the carpet could easily mask any sign of violence or bloodshed. I knew there were notorious bootleggers among us, but what had Claudia so on edge? She kept glancing at the discreetly hidden side doors as if expecting danger to burst through at any moment, bringing with it a storm of chaos and destruction.

Claudia was usually the picture of confidence when surrounded by her friends, but now she seemed like a frightened animal backed into a corner. We, her friends and I, were all on our way to help the suffrage movement take a step forward. Well…I also joined in order to secure good whiskey. So, why did she seem paranoid and protective, as if she was the target of some murder plot?

"What's going on?" I demanded, my voice low and urgent as I leaned in close to her ear. Making sure it was her good ear, I'd made the mistake of whispering in her deaf ear before and realized she couldn't hear me at all. Her eyes, usually bright and full of joy, now looked weary and sad as she turned to face me. We were squeezed together in a small club chair, but I couldn't focus on anything other than her distress. All I wanted was to make her happy, to see her dazzling smile light up every part of me again. But for now, it seemed like all I could do was hold her and try to ease her pain.

She let out a deep, frustrated sigh. "There's been a rumor," she began, her voice trembling with anger and fear. "A rumor that's completely gotten under my skin." She looked around nervously, her body shaking ever so slightly. Without hesitation, I wrapped my arms around her, wanting to provide any comfort I could.

"What kind of rumor?" I asked, digging through my brain for any clue that could lead to what could be causing her such fear. While gossip can cause apprehension, Claudia seemed physically frightened.

Her next words sent a chill down my spine. "A group of men in my mother's circle have launched an anti-suffrage campaign." My heart dropped as she spoke the words. The thought of anyone trying to block women's right to vote filled me with rage. "And if we ever do get the right to vote," Claudia continued, her voice strained with emotion, "they plan to watch the polls and intimidate women. They've even shown up at suffragette parades with violence." She quickly scanned our surroundings once again, as if afraid that someone might hear her.

My blood boiled at the thought of men using fear and violence to silence women's voices. And seeing Claudia so shaken by this news only fueled my fury further. Together, we sat there in tense silence, holding each other tightly.

"It's a good thing you brought your loyal guard dog with you." I raised my eyebrow, the corner of my mouth twitching upwards, as Claudia's dazzling smile lit up her face. Just then, a tall, shadowy figure stepped out from the darkness and fixed his intense gaze on Claudia. Instinctively, I pulled her closer to me for protection.

Florian bounded over to us, brimming with excitement, completely unaware. "I brought matching hats for all of us to wear at the rally. You're going to love them." She playfully grabbed Claudia's face and planted a quick peck on her rosy cheek. Claudia couldn't help but smile despite her trepidation, but she squeezed my arm all the same.

"Absolutely," Kiersten chimed in, joining our little group. "And it would be even better if we could celebrate with some good whiskey." She winked at me before turning to beam at Claudia and Florian. Lina joined us then too, her expression mirroring the unease that had been plaguing Claudia. With a subtle nod towards a cluster of men, including the shadowy figure in the corner of the room, Lina hinted at their shady intentions. They were just beyond a group of elegantly dressed women in low-waisted beaded dresses and tuxedo-clad men, but they instead donned tweed vests and flat caps, like my usual crew, creating an intriguing contrast among the partygoers.

They didn't seem like the guys from Claudia's mother's circle. Could they be hired out? "They seem like trouble," Lina said to us. And the cloud that had been over Claudia returned. The group of men appeared completely out of their element. They kept fidgeting and adjusting their collars, trying to look tough. They better not be here for the same barrels I'm after.

"Why don't I go tell them hello and try to find out more about them?" I asked. Florian and Kiersten smiled; perhaps they were inwardly hoping I'd invite the guys over. It was as if they were sharing a silent secret, but I wasn't sure what it was. I really hoped they didn't have any interest because I'd been wishing they were attracted to James and Thomas.

It would be nice to have the whole group able to go out on dates together, and it might help move things along for me and Claudia. We could be each other's chaperones.

"Be careful," Claudia cautioned, her voice low and urgent.

Lina's eyes flickered with concern as she added, "Try to see if they have any interest in the rally, or if they're here for something completely different."

"Well then, I'm off." Taking a deep breath, I squeezed Claudia's arm softly for reassurance before stepping away.

Adjusting my vest and running a hand through my hair, I made my way towards the group of men. Past the beaded dresses and tuxedos, I wondered how my approach would be met. One of the men had a cigarette hanging from his mouth and was patting his pockets in search of a light. I pulled the matchbox out of my pocket.

"Need a light?" I offered.

"Yeah thanks, man." He leaned forward as I lit a match and held it out. His hair was shaved close from the ears down and his nose was a little crooked, as if it had been broken more than once. "Name's Arthur."

"I'm Alex." We shook hands.

He inhaled and released a puff of smoke. "What do you think about all of the eggs around here?" He gestured to the posh crowd around us. I smirked and shook my head, trying to win his trust a bit. The thought of him having a connection to Claudia's mother was diminishing by the second.

One by one, the men shook my hand; each with firm grips full of calluses. The man in the middle avoided eye contact, his gaze fixed on something in the distance. When I followed his line of sight, all I saw was the glistening blue water in the sunlight.

"What brings you aboard with this boring group of upper-class?" I hedged.

"Just a boys' trip," the man on the left who introduced himself as Michael proclaimed, slapping the middle companion on the back.

"Not looking to score a few barrels of anything?" Were they bootleggers like me?

"No, we're more the basketeering type than barrel chasing, if you know what I mean." Arthur laughed out, his voice rough and deep as he looked me up and down.

"Okay," I hesitated, not sure what they were talking about.

Suddenly, I heard footsteps approaching from behind me. Florian and Kiersten appeared at my side, their presence calming my nerves. "We came over to see what was taking so long," Florian said with a smile.

Arthur turned to Florian and Kiersten, a mischievous glint in his eye. "Are you two fans of seafood?" he asked.

Florian's face lit up with excitement. "How did you know?" she giggled.

I stood there, feeling completely lost as the conversation continued on in this strange language.

"Wait, are you here with Athenaeum?" Kiersten prodded.

The man in the middle, who introduced himself as John, grinned, removed his cap, and then bowed dramatically. "The one and only," he declared. He did have an attractive demeanor. His hair was styled with a voluminous side part and his eyes lit up when he smiled, giving him a boyish look.

Florian squealed, grabbed John's and Michael's hands while Kiersten snatched Arthur's as well as mine. They pulled us all back to the group.

"Are they really here to help with the rally?" Lina asked skeptically, eyeing the newcomers suspiciously.

"Why, of course," Michael replied with a charming smile. "We believe in equality for all." He winked at Florian, who smiled back.

I wasn't sure if they could be trusted, but with the mention of Athenaeum, these guys had won the full trust of the girls. Standing next to Claudia, I could feel her tension release slightly. But her trust would not be so easily achieved, and I admired her more for it.

"What's Athenaeum?" I asked Claudia.

"It's the largest Kansas City Women's club," Claudia responded with a smirk. "Not only are they strongly woven into the national group, but they have plenty of connections like newspaper journalists too. It's actually quite marvelous how they intricately advocate progressive reforms for suppressed groups."

A sudden burst of commotion near the grand entryway of the salon caught everyone's attention. All eyes turned to see the arrival of Sylvester Swan, a singer known for his opulent taste and extravagant lifestyle. The double French doors opened wide, revealing a figure draped in luxurious silks and adorned with sparkling jewels. He glided into the room, commanding attention with each step. The chatter of guests hushed as they watched him make his way through the crowd, his presence filling the space with an air of elegance and poise.

Sylvester, with his underdog story, was the designated provider of entertainment for the trip. His entourage of musicians and performers followed closely behind, instruments at the ready. The sound of their lively chatter and tinkling tambourines could be heard from afar. With every step he took, Sylvester's confidence radiated like a beacon. He was a true showman, ready to dazzle and delight with his talents on this journey.

Florian, Kiersten, and the Athenaeum guys all grasped one another in awe, their eyes wide with excitement. "We have to watch him perform," Florian exclaimed, her voice filled with wonder.

John nodded eagerly, his face alight with anticipation. "Wouldn't miss it for the world."

"You all have fun," Lina interjected, her tone slightly reserved. "I'm going to sit this one out."

Kiersten pouted playfully, her bottom lip rolling into a mock frown. "Please?"

"No, really, I have some calculations to work on," Lina persisted.

"We can walk you to your room," I offered. "If that's all right with you?" I turned to Claudia for confirmation.

"Yes, I'm actually beat all of a sudden and could use some downtime."

I smiled at Claudia, glad she seemed to read my mind.

"Fine, but you're going to miss the show of a lifetime." Florian teased, then hugged Lina, Claudia, and me. "Take care of my girls," she instructed me.

"I'll tell you all about it tomorrow." Kiersten also hugged us good night.

I pulled John aside. "Watch out for them, will you?"

"Of course, it's my honor."

With that, the Athenaeum men and the girls followed the crowd while Lina, Claudia, and I made our way towards the room compartments. Lina seemed to breathe a sigh of relief as the door to the front lounge shut behind us. I feared how she'd handle the rally if she's not one for crowds. Once we neared Lina's room, she turned to bid us farewell.

"Thank you for the escort. I need to make sure we have enough sashes and, if not, get ahold of the leaders for more in time. Plus, there are the pamphlets to consider."

"Of course. Would you like some help?" Claudia offered.

"No, no, you know how I am with my calculations. Best leave me alone."

"All right, well, good night." Claudia hugged Lina.

As we continued down the hallway towards Claudia's room, she turned to me with a gentle smile. "Would you like to come in for a bit?"

"Alone? Are you sure?" I asked, slightly taken aback by her offer but excited all the same.

"Of course!" She opened the door and ushered me inside, a sly grin spreading across her face.

Pouring water into two glasses from a nearby pitcher, Claudia motioned for me to take a seat on the small sofa that barely fit in the cramped space. The room was cluttered with a vanity at one end and a dresser at the other, leaving little room for walking. Despite the cramped quarters, Claudia seemed perfectly at ease as she sat cross-legged on one end of the sofa, not caring about being ladylike. Something about it brought me happiness, her being so comfortable around me.

"So, that was quite an eventful start to our trip," she remarked with a raised eyebrow and a playful smile.

"It was. Do you think Florian and Kiersten will be all right?"

"Yes, yes," Claudia reassured me before taking a sip of water. "They'll manage just fine."

"I must say, your room is thoroughly nice," I commented, looking around at the simple but cozy space.

Claudia let out a small laugh. "No, it's not, but it's not the worst either."

"True," I agreed, thinking back to my own small, shared room, with bunk beds and minimal furnishings.

"I'm glad we finally have some time alone."

"You are?" Most women would find it scandalous, but I was quickly realizing just how independent and forward-thinking Claudia was.

Armored Hours

Chapter Six - Marie

Hansen 63

Let's cut to the chase. Claudia and her friends are on a trip, and I'm left here with a gnawing worry for their safety. But as I watch my daughter experience true joy, surrounded by her closest companions, I can't help but feel grateful for these rare moments of happiness amidst the chaos.

Yet, in this new body I'm trapped in, I must play the role of a wealthy socialite, forced to endure the company of vultures who only crave my money. It's sickening how easily they swarm around me, like scavengers in the desert.

And it's even more unsettling to see Claudia and her friends fighting for women's rights while knowing that in the future, those same rights will be taken away and given back like a disposable toy. The irony of having memories from a different time is that I'm acutely aware of the impending doom facing us. It's a blessing and a curse that both Claudia and my sister have neither, memories from past lives or future ones.

I wish I could send my daughter to meet Audre Lorde, to learn from her wisdom and strength. But alas, she has not yet been born in this timeline. And even though she will make an impact during Claudia's lifetime, her revolutionary work will not be recognized until much later.

Audre would tell my daughter that we cannot use the tools of our oppressors to break free from their grasp. But by the time we realize this hard truth, it may already be too late. Yet, despite the looming darkness ahead, I find solace in seeing Claudia and her friends standing up for what they believe in and holding their ground against oppression. Especially when Kiersten and Florian join them in their fight for queer rights. They will need every ounce of strength they can muster as they face an uphill battle against ignorance and hate.

The silver beams of the full moon dance across the rippling surface of the pond, casting a mystical glow upon our meeting spot for the invocation. Nelly graciously agreed to invite her friend Anna, who also accepted our invitation. Though we are not sisters in this particular timeline, she still holds a special place in my heart. I could spot those clever and artistic eyes from yards away, and as Nelly walks her around, introducing her to everyone, I can't help but pay special attention to her every movement.

Her mannerisms are just as I remember them, unwavering and graceful. But unlike me, she does not possess memories of our shared past and future. As an anomaly in this timeline, I was both blessed and burdened with this knowledge. When I take Anna's hand in mine, a flicker of recognition crosses her face and, for a moment, I begin to doubt myself. Does she have hidden memories of the future? If so, she should be terrified...unless the timeline has been altered by another's actions. Perhaps her soulmate throughout time has also caused a fork in her path, just like he had with his. Shaking off these thoughts, I brush my hand through my hair to steady myself. It wouldn't do to scare her away before I'm able to learn more.

Once everyone is properly introduced, we form a circle around the crackling fire by the pond. I'm standing to the north, while Nelly stands to the west (after whispering instructions to Anna even though she's familiar with the practice through some of her employees), Olinda to the east, and Anna to the south. We each raise our hands towards the sky as we began our invocation.

"Oh, once there was a little girl whose tears dripped into ponds of sorrow," I sing out first, ending my lines on the ethereal notes of e and a. Invoking the Goddess Eras.

"Follow all couples," Olinda's voice rises next, invoking Morrigan with her arms outstretched. "For it is the way of promises and vows to soon let us down." The Goddess Morrigan is well known for moving spirits through cycles.

Anna's voice joins in; just as beautiful as I remember it, invoking Cerridwen with her own unique melody. "Oh, once there was a ceremony that bound one another forever, but only half of those bonds were meant to last, taking them away for always." The Goddess Cerridwen is known for her knowledge and inspiration.

Nelly finishes the sequence with her own invocation of Brigid, her voice low and commanding. "Be quiet," she warns us, "for secrets prove to be misadventures. And all still circled the pond, which had pooled only heartbreak and gallows." With our invocations complete, we stand in silence for a moment before breaking into song and dance, celebrating the power and wisdom of the Goddesses who watch over us.

With an excitedly shaking hand, I offer each of them a necklace adorned with a triquetra pendant. My mind races as I contemplate how to fix this dire situation. Should I attempt to send a message to a past life, the very first one where he took my sister from me? But what consequences would it bring? I had dabbled in sorcery before, using verbal poetry to incant reincarnation. But messing with time and fate always comes with a heavy price.

But something changed in the future, allowing him to spawn back twice over. While the rest of us have only one clear path in our past, he has caused his pathway to fork into two treacherous roads. Can I stop him from taking this destructive course without causing damage to transmigration lines? As I focus my gaze, I can see two timelines dangerously close together, closer than ever before, with no generational gaps. The mere thought of changing one causes a violent vibration to erupt, whipping everyone's hair back despite standing in a circle.

In the first close timeline, his power allowed him to travel between worlds with just a thought, but it left a tethered string trailing behind like a curse. That shining thread was necessary for his escape from that other world in the first place. But how did he break free far into the future? And how did the rest of us manage to escape as well? Was it because of that same shiny string that now seems to have returned here with us? The past, present, and future timelines are all tangled and chaotic.

My relentless study and research have led me full circle, right back to where we started. We must find his twin lifelines and put an end to their destruction before it's too late. That's why I asked Nelly to cast protection spells on the necklaces before giving them out. It brings some comfort knowing my sister will always be protected by the powerful charm.

Olinda's eyes sparkle as she shares her latest accomplishments with us. "I've sent help to the suffrage movement," she announces proudly.

"Thank you for sending assistance with the girls," I gratefully reply, thinking of how kind it was of Olinda to involve the Athenaeum in safeguarding my daughter and her friends. Despite our busy lives, we make an effort to gather together once every moon cycle and catch up. If only I could convince my daughter to visit more often, I could bestow upon her a powerful protection charm.

"Well, you know what they say about being well-connected." I wink mischievously. "I happen to be friends with the mother of a member of the Tennessee state legislature."

Genuine applause erupts from our circle as Olinda shares another achievement: a hidden safehouse on her land where battered women and their children can find refuge. But among the celebration, there is also concern. "The government is looking to tax me more," Olinda reveals with a frown.

"They seem to be doing that a lot lately," Anna says.

But Nelly, always quick with a solution, speaks up with confidence. "I can see into the future, and I believe you're about to come into some money!" She even rubs her palm on her thigh to prove it. "We have friends who are always looking to flaunt their wealth and throw their money around."

A sly smile spreads across Olinda's face as she considers this offer. "Well, as long as your methods work in my favor, I say we have a deal."

One by one, we take turns sharing our own successes and accomplishments. Anna, in awe of Nelly's abilities, asks incredulously, "You're a successful business owner, a fortune teller, and also have time to be a doula?"

Nelly beams with pride and nods confidently. "Yes, my volunteer work as a doula has been very successful with the women in our community." As we continue to share and support each other, I can't help but feel grateful for the amazing friends I have. And as I look at Anna's beaming smile, I see glimpses of my own sister, making me miss her even more.

My words are laced with sarcasm as I remark, "Nelly always manages to find trouble when she's bored." She kicks dirt in my direction and we all laugh, comradery hanging in the air.

"Thank you all for being here and for your efforts to make a better future," I say. As I finish my statement, a chilling vision of the distant future floods my mind. It's nearly 250 years from now and my daughter stands before me, brimming with strength and determination as if she heard our invocation. Is she readying herself for battle?

"Are you okay?" Nelly's voice jolts me back to the present. I hadn't even noticed her approach until I felt her hand on my arm, concern etched on her face.

"I'm fine," I lie, unable to shake off the unsettling images in my mind.

"We should probably leave before we're caught," Olinda interjects, breaking the tense moment. "We don't want another Salem Witch Trials on our hands."

But Anna's dry humor cuts through the unease like a knife. "More like The Red Scare," she quips, earning a nervous laugh from us all. As we walk away from the peaceful pond, my mind races with thoughts of my daughter and what kind of battle she will face in the future. How is it connected to the troubling events happening in our own time? Fear and uncertainty grip me as we make our hasty retreat.

CHAPTER SEVEN – CLAUDIA

OFFICIAL PROGRAM
WOMAN SUFFRAGE
PROCESSION
"HOW LONG MUST WOMEN
WAIT FOR FREEDOM?"

Claudia shifted closer to Alex on the plush sofa in her room aboard THE MISSOURI, her eyes sparkling with curiosity.

"Tell me something I don't know about you," she whispered, as if they were sharing secrets in a crowded room.

Alex mirrored her movement, inching closer, as he thought of his answer. "I've already told you about my ma and brother."

"What about your da?" Claudia pressed further, her hand gently resting on his knee.

Alex exhaled, steeling himself, before answering. "They were like two pieces of a puzzle that fit perfectly together. It made me sick to watch as a boy—how they finished each other's sentences and moved in perfect sync. My ma would be cooking and my da would seamlessly hand her ingredients just as she needed them. And my ma could anticipate his needs too, picking up a tube of paint from the store before he even realized it was running low."

He paused, his voice catching slightly. "But they were complete opposites too. He was drawn to the thrill of danger and art, while she preferred the simple pleasure of fresh cut peppers and pulled daisies in a vase. As a kid, I longed for some time away from their sappy love. But now...now I realize it was special." A hint of sadness crept into his tone. "Especially since he's gone."

Claudia's delicate hand reached up to Alex's cheek, her warm touch comforting his troubled heart. Her thumb brushed away a single tear that had escaped his notice, and in that small gesture, he found solace. Drawing in a deep breath, he tried to push away the bittersweet memories that threatened to consume him.

"What about you?" he asked, needing a distraction from his thoughts.

She withdrew her hand, leaving behind the warmth that he craved. "Oh, me? Well, you know who my mother is, right?" Her words were laced with bitterness, and he could see the pain etched into her features.

"I've gathered," he replied carefully. "But what about your father?"

A shadow passed over her face, darkening the light in her hazel eyes. A part of him regretted bringing up the subject, recognizing the familiar discomfort in her expression. But another part couldn't resist the curiosity and longing to connect with this wondrous woman before him—strong, kind, and full of secrets.

"My father was a formidable guardian of my mother and myself. He exuded an atmosphere of strength and protection. My mother, surrounded by her tight-knit group of friends, seemed to dance to the rhythm of a different tune. And my father, always inquisitive and curious about the world around him, was constantly trying to uncover its secrets."

But ever since his passing, my mother has looked at me with a wary gaze, as if expecting me to transform into some kind of monster. Or perhaps she's just filling the void left in his absence by trying to marry me off to the most eligible bachelor. It's all interwoven with the societal charade that I have no interest in being a part of." She sighed. "Sorry for bringing up such a somber topic."

As Claudia finished speaking, Alex gently placed his hand on her cheek, cradling her face tenderly. She managed a small smile through the lingering unease of the memories before composing herself again. Her eyes darted down to Alex's lips for a split second before returning to meet his gaze.

Their lips met in a soft, delicate kiss, and a bubble of heat surrounded Alex and Claudia. Desperately wanting more, Alex tangled his hands through Claudia's hair, pulling her closer for another kiss. Their hearts beat as one and their bodies hummed with desire.

With one hand now resting on the nape of her neck, Alex pulled away, his dilated eyes meeting Claudia's. "That was…amazing," he said, struggling to find words that expressed the intensity of their connection.

All Claudia could do was nod in agreement, her own breaths coming in short gasps as the fire between them begged to be stoked further. As Alex started to speak again, she grabbed him in an ardent embrace, not wanting to hear anything that might ruin this moment. In that instant, it was hard for even Claudia to know whether it was precisely because she didn't want to hear his next words or if her own desires were clouding her judgment. But she knew one thing—they wanted each other.

They wrapped their arms around one another as their bodies communicated their need; Claudia was flushed with desire. Alex knew it was flirting with disaster, being alone in her room like this, doing what they were doing. Allowing this passion to continue unbridled would be absolute chaos, and yet he couldn't deny the deeply intoxicating pull Claudia had on him.

"Don't leave," Claudia whispered quietly, as if reading his mind.

"Never," Alex replied without hesitation.

"Stay with me," she pleaded, moving so their bodies could be closer.

"It goes against all etiquette, though," he hesitated.

"As if I care," Claudia asserted firmly.

For a moment, Alex's breath caught in his throat at her words, slicing through to his core. In front of him lay the woman he was falling hard for, and he couldn't bear the thought of leaving her tonight.

Without another word, he curled up beside her as she sleepily nestled into his embrace. Gently, he brushed a strand of hair away from her face and tucked it behind her ear. Claudia grabbed his hand and pulled his arm over her, seeking comfort and warmth in his touch, wanting him even closer. They sunk into the velvet of the sofa, cocooned in warmth.

As the emotions of the day ran through them—fear juxtaposing elation—everything became swiftly calm as they lay there together. Drifting off to sleep, they found peaceful contentment in each other's arms.

The next morning, their blissful slumber was interrupted by a loud knock at the door. It was Lina calling out from the other side. "You're usually the one up early. It's time to go!" she said, interrupting their precious moment of rest together. "We need to catch the Dixie Flyer."

Claudia's voice echoed through the hallway as she called out to Lina, "Be right out. Meet you at the front lounge."

"I can wait," Lina replied, her voice slightly muffled through the door. "Hate being there by myself."

Claudia quickly brushed through her hair with her fingers and splashed some cool water on her face before smoothing out the wrinkles in her clothes. She flashed a smile at Alex, hoping he didn't mind waiting a bit longer before leaving. "Mind waiting until after Lina and I go to the lounge?"

He could see the worry in her eyes about their reputation. He hoped this didn't mean that their passionate night together would be forgotten. But he understood she had obligations and responsibilities, and he couldn't keep her from them. Still, the thought of not holding her again for a long time caused a small pang in his chest.

It was a flurry as Alex grabbed his hat, preparing to leave as soon as the coast was clear and collect his rucksack from his quarters. Claudia's hand grasping his caused him to pause. She leaned in and kissed him on the cheek. "See you soon," she whispered.

He watched her leave with a sense of longing. Once she closed the door behind her, he heard Lina chatter excitedly about their upcoming plans as they walked away. Claudia grasped onto Lina with excitement in her eyes she couldn't explain.

"We'll catch the train, and our mentors will meet us when we arrive in Nashville." Lina refolded the letter in her hands and looked at Claudia. "What has you so joyful? Finally sleep without nightmares?"

"No nightmares, just dream after dream." Claudia smiled, thinking of the kiss with Alex.

"It's about time. No wonder you slept in."

As they approached Kiersten's and Florian's door, they heard jubilant voices. It opened before Claudia could even knock. Two of the Athenaeum men, Michael and John, exited first. They were draped onto each other in what looked to be a hungover haze. Kiersten and Florian exited next; arms clasped together.

Lina cleared her throat, shooting them a disapproving look. "Could you at least try to be less conspicuous?"

"What's the big deal? Nothing happened last night, and you know it," Florian protested.

"It's not me I'm worried about," Lina shot back.

"Whoever is dimwitted or nosy enough to pass undeserving judgment, I'm not interested in having their favor, anyway," Kiersten interjected with a shrug.

Claudia remained silent. It's not like she could rightfully tell them to change their behavior, considering what she had done the previous evening. But she also didn't want to face Lina's wrath, knowing how protective she was and how much danger their friends could be in if the wrong person saw them.

With a flick of her wrist, Lina gave instructions to the bellhops to collect their things. Florian, cigarette in hand, stood off to the side as the group huddled together in their own little bubble. Tensions had been high just moments before, but now there was a sense of comfort and familiarity among them, like a family coming together after a disagreement.

"We're in the same car as you, but were unable to secure adjoining seats," the Athenaeum leader, Arthur, said.

"That's okay, darling," Florian remarked, ever the charismatic one. "You know sign language, right?"

He knocked the air twice with his fist indicating, "yes."

"Great, we can talk from afar." Kiersten playfully winked at him.

Claudia watched the exchange with a swell of pride in her chest. She couldn't help but feel grateful for this makeshift family she had found.

Alex ran up to them, rucksack in tow.

"Want the bellhop to add your bag with our stuff?" Lina asked.

"No, no, I'm all right." Alex pulled the strap higher on his shoulder. Claudia could tell he was feeling jittery and placed a comforting hand on his arm. He exhaled and then smiled at her.

Following the instructions of the steamboat staff, they disembarked onto the bustling dock. Bellhops with round hats hurried past them as other passengers milled about, creating a lively atmosphere. The anticipation of their journey ahead filled them all with excitement and energy.

As they approached the main road, the leader of the Athenaeum gestured towards a sleek Renault parked by the curb. "Our ride is over here," he announced. "It'll take us to the train station in time for boarding."

Lina's brow furrowed in concern. "Um, minor problem. That won't seat all of us," she interjected. "We should have stuck to my original plan."

"I can add a couple more to my ride," Alex offered, pointing to an older Model T Ford nearby. It was clearly not as luxurious as the Renault, but it would fit the stragglers.

"Sounds good to me," Claudia said, linking her arm with Alex's.

"Our escapade continues." Florian grinned at the sight of the two vehicles, taking Kiersten's hand in her own.

"Guess that puts me with you two," Lina said, joining Claudia and Alex in the Model T.

Throughout the car ride, Claudia tried to distract Lina from her frustrations by pointing out different styles of building architecture and making light-hearted jokes. But

Lina's mood remained sour. Finally, Claudia couldn't take it any longer and asked, "What's wrong?"

"I just don't like how dangerous this all is," Lina confided in a hushed tone. "You never know when a bigot with a gun could show up. I wish we could be worry free."

Claudia wrapped her arm around her friend in a comforting hug, both of them falling silent as they caught their first glimpse of the train station ahead. Stone archways lined the building and scaffolding rose in front of them, as if constructing peaks for some grand cathedral. "This is the largest American railroad terminal," Lina marveled in awe at the St. Louis Union Station.

Climbing up the stairs to the Dixie Flyer, each gentleman took a lady's hand to assist. Kiersten, who usually brushed off such chivalrous gestures, couldn't help but accept it from these men. After all, they were embarking on a journey to advocate for women's right to vote.

Inside, they were immediately struck by the decadent wood paneling and the plush, cushioned seats. It felt like stepping into a different world, one of luxury and privilege. Once everyone was settled in their seats, Alex excused himself to go to his designated section. However, Claudia wasn't ready to let him go just yet. She grabbed his hand and questioned where he was headed.

"Uh, I don't have a ticket for this car," Alex explained.

"Hold on, just a moment," she said.

She noticed the seat beside her just so happened to be open, but she needed to act quickly.

"Well, you do now." Claudia winked at him before pulling the conductor aside and whispering something in his ear. She then slipped some money into his palm and returned to Alex with a triumphant smile. "I just upgraded your ticket."

Feeling a mixture of gratitude and embarrassment by Claudia's gesture, Alex took the seat beside her.

CHAPTER EIGHT – ALEX

THE DIXIE FLYER
ALL STEEL TRAINS
ALL YEAR ROUND
THE SCENIC ROUTE
FINEST AND MOST COMPREHENSIVE SERVICE

As we settled into our seats, Claudia's smile faded and her grip tightened on my arm. She leaned in close, using her thumb to point discreetly behind her. With silent urgency, she mouthed the words "it's him."

Trying to appear nonchalant, I peered over her shoulder towards the back window and the cheaper seats outside. The figure wearing a flat cap seemed vaguely familiar, but in my line of work, those were a common sight. It wasn't until he turned his head that I recognized who it was—my arch nemesis, Kris Mardell. His profile was one that I could never forget, having seen it numerous times in extracted police records.

"Kris Mardell?" I confirmed Claudia's fears, and she shuddered beside me.

I instinctively put my arm around her, offering comfort, as she nuzzled into the crook of my neck. She was trembling with fear. Perhaps her earlier unease aboard THE MISSOURI had been more than just a feeling. Maybe her intuition had picked up on something I had missed. She knew there was trouble brewing and thought it had been resolved when we identified the Athenaeum men. But now, lurking behind the veil of camouflage, was our real enemy.

Could he be here for the same whiskey that I was after? He'd better not be. While he may have mistreated a woman at the Chamberlain Resort, I didn't think he would dare target someone as high-profile as Claudia. That would bring far too much unwanted attention his way. So, what was his purpose for being here? Was he paid by someone else to do a different kind of job? If so, what could that job possibly be?

Kiersten and Florian were silently communicating with the Athenaeum men, using the same method Kiersten and Claudia had used before the raid. As I observed their interactions, an idea struck me like a bolt of lightning. With the men sitting closer to Kris, I leaned in and whispered to Claudia, "Can they try to eavesdrop on Kris's conversation through the window?"

Claudia quickly signaled to the girls, who relayed the message to the men. It was invigorating to see them working as a team, especially since we outnumbered Kris. He only had one companion, while there were eight of us. Even Claudia seemed to relax slightly, surveying our group with a newfound sense of confidence. As the waiter approached to take our orders, I was grateful that we had coordinated beforehand.

It was difficult to discuss our plans with Kris's presence looming over us, but the promise of tea seemed to calm Lina and even allowed Claudia to lean against me for support. I couldn't believe she was showing me such affection. Someone of her status shouldn't be giving me any attention, especially in public.

As soon as the room cleared out a bit and the men had eavesdropped on some of Kris's conversation, Claudia leaned in close and whispered to me what they had heard. "It seems he's after the same thing you are," she said with a worried expression etched on her face.

I felt my heart sink at this disheartening news. "I'll have to act quickly once we arrive," I responded, already dreading the distance that would separate us at our destination.

"Do you remember our rendezvous plans?" Claudia asked.

I nodded firmly.

"Should we have the Athenaeum men accompany you?" she inquired, concern evident in her voice.

Despite her worry for my safety, I knew that it would be better for her to have extra protection at the rally, given the fact that some of her own societal peers were planning to launch an anti-suffrage movement. "No, I can handle Kris on my own," I assured her with determination.

"Okay," she agreed with a hint of reluctance, but still held onto my arm tightly, as if wanting to provide some sort of protection.

As we approached Nashville, my heart began to pound in anticipation. The tall clock tower loomed ahead, a symbol of the bustling city and our destination. Thomas, through our contact in Tennessee named Adam, had provided me with the password to secure the coveted whiskey I was after. I felt grateful for his longstanding relationship with Thomas, knowing that Kris wouldn't be able to obtain it without that connection.

Lina, as always, provided information to the group as we arrived at the station. "Our mentors will meet us here," she said. "We're going straight to the rally."

I could see Claudia's nerves getting the best of her as she wrung her hands. "You're going to do great," I reassured her.

"I'm just so anxious," she admitted.

I took her hands in mine and looked into her anxious eyes with a comforting smile. She smiled back, despite her trepidation. Then, remembering a relaxation technique, I applied pressure between her thumb and forefinger. "There's a pressure point here," I explained. "If you squeeze it, it will help take your body's focus away from nervousness or pain."

"Thank you," she said, leaning in to kiss me on the cheek.

As we made our way through another bustling crowd once again, a group of women dressed in long white dresses and white shoes approached Lina. They welcomed us to Nashville and offered to escort us to the Suffragette headquarters.

"I hope your trip wasn't too stressful," the leader of the group said. "We have a busy afternoon ahead. Do you have the sashes and pamphlets to add to our inventory?"

"Yes," Lina confirmed confidently. "I double checked my calculations on the way here."

"Wonderful," the leader replied. Then, turning to Claudia, she asked if she was ready for her speech.

Claudia nodded, and I gave her a side hug for support. As I did, I caught sight of Kris and his companion entering a nearby vehicle. I knew I had to act quickly.

My heart raced as I reassured Claudia, knowing that I was leaving her vulnerable and alone in a dangerous situation. "You'll be okay," I told her, trying to convince myself as well. "You've got this."

She looked at me with sadness in her eyes. "Too bad you have to go," she said regretfully. "I wish you could be there with me."

"Me too," I replied, my thoughts already consumed by the potential danger awaiting me when I left. "But I've got to make sure Kris doesn't mess up my plans."

"Be careful," she warned, her voice filled with uneasiness.

"You too, doll," I said, testing my new nickname for her before reluctantly leaving her side. Having to be away from Claudia was becoming one of my least favorite things, but Kris didn't allow any room for hesitation or delay.

As I made my way through the crowded streets, I noticed someone wearing a flat cap in the driver's seat of the vehicle my crew had left for me. My instincts immediately kicked in, and I ducked behind someone in the crowd. Making my way towards the back of the car, I crouched low so as not to be seen.

My heart pounded in my chest as I peered into the side mirror, trying to discern who was sitting in the driver's seat. As they turned to face the mirror, relief flooded over me.

I stood up and cautiously approached the driver's side window, knocking to get their attention.

Adam rolled down the window and smiled at me. "Hey mate," he greeted me casually.

"Adam? I wasn't expecting to see you here," I said in surprise.

"Well, I figured why not join in on the fun?" he replied with a smirk. "And it seems like you have quite a tale, or should I say tail."

I followed his nod towards where Kris and his friend were still sitting in their car, their eyes trained directly on me. I turned back to Adam with frustration and anger coursing through my veins. "For crying out loud, someone needs to tell them to beat it!"

Adam's expression turned serious as he leaned in closer to me. "Word on the street is that Kris is waiting for you to secure the whiskey so he can jump you and take it."

My teeth ground together, a growl bubbling up from my throat at the thought of Kris' treacherous plans. I took a deep, steadying breath and braced myself for whatever dangers lay ahead. It was shaping up to be a day filled with tension and peril.

Adam and I drove in tense silence, wracking our brains for a way to outmaneuver Kris. We weaved through the city streets, avoiding our actual destination as more roads were blocked off by rally traffic and barriers. I was able to glimpse the Capitol building through a main street and for a second admire its careful craftsmanship and artistry as well as the cupola.

"This is going to be tough," Adam grunted, staring out at the chaotic scene.

And then I saw it—a distant stage, adorned with ribbons and a large banner. But what caught my eye was the figure standing at the microphone. Claudia. She was giving an impassioned speech that echoed through the streets, her voice ringing with conviction and fire.

"We will not stand for any neglect or dismissal of women's rights and needs! We must present a united front and show that no political party can ignore us!" Her words were like a rallying cry, empowering and fierce.

I felt a surge of pride and admiration for this remarkable woman who had shown me vulnerability just moments ago. Now she stood before me as a mighty force, shining brighter than I'd ever seen her before. She was a true marvel, and I knew without a doubt that she would lead women to victory.

Adam's tap on my arm pulled me out of my thoughts and back into the present moment. With a quick glance, I confirmed that Kris was no longer in sight. "Do you think we lost him?" I asked, heart pounding in my chest.

"I'll circle around a block on the way to be sure," Adam replied, his voice tense with apprehension.

I looked around frantically, scanning every corner for any sign of Kris or his companion. But they seemed to have vanished into thin air. It all felt too easy. After traveling all this way with such determination, why would Kris give up so easily?

But there was no time to dwell on my suspicions. The rendezvous time to meet Claudia was approaching, and I didn't want to risk being late.

"I think the coast is clear," Adam finally said, breaking the silence. I just nodded in agreement as we drove a few more miles until the warehouse came into view.

Exiting the car cautiously, I couldn't shake off the feeling that Kris could still be lurking somewhere, waiting to pounce. My nerves were on edge when I should have been focusing on preparing myself to meet one of the biggest bootleggers in the country who happened to be in town to distribute the last batch of whiskey before it was confiscated by authorities.

Adam led me through a side door into a dark and musky room filled with crates and equipment. We wound our way through until he opened a large, wooden sliding door and revealed an opulent office space. Every piece of furniture exuded luxury with intricate woodwork and decadent lighting. The musty smell from earlier had disappeared completely.

"Alex, I'm so glad you could make it," a man in an expensive burgundy suit greeted us as he stood up from behind his desk. He extended his hand for a shake.

Feeling underdressed and out of place, I nervously returned the handshake. "It's an honor to meet you, Mr. Remus," I replied, trying to sound confident and at ease.

"Please, call me George," he said and motioned to the seat in front of the desk while he sat in the one behind it. "There have been rumblings throughout the Midwest of your precision to detail. I hear you're mostly selling the top shelf stuff."

"Well, comes hand in hand when dealing with some of the most brilliant minds in the business." I winked at him.

"Do tell Anna hello for me." He smiled and then snapped his fingers. Adam grabbed a crystal decanter off the shelf and poured into two matching crystal glasses, handing one to George and one to me. Oh, this was the moment to prove who I was.

We tapped our glasses together, and George lifted his eyebrows. Luckily, the passphrase came rushing forward. "To the unfettered control of our own destinies."

"Salute." George smiled and relief washed over me. Adam joined us with a drink of his own, and we discussed the logistics loading the barrels in a covered luggage trailer, the specific route to take back to the train, and the people to speak to at the train station as well as the boat crew.

After the whirlwind of discussion settled, Adam and I got to the task at hand of attaching and loading the trailer. It was hard work, but that wasn't uncommon for me. Plus, Adam was a funny guy to be around, and he helped the time pass quickly. I was worried about sticking to the timeline for meeting at the scheduled rendezvous, and I lifted my head to tell Adam just that when I noticed his eyes were as big as saucers and his mouth agape. When he held his hands in the air, my heart dropped to my stomach.

I turned around to see Kris and his companion. The companion held a gun in Adam's direction while Kris pointed one at me.

"Don't be stupid, Kris," I scoffed. "This inventory is intended for a specific location and a lot of people in big places will be upset if their customer isn't satisfied. You won't make it a week, no matter how far you run."

"When I want your opinion, I'll ask for it." Before I could respond, he hit me upside the head with the butt of his gun, and I faltered on my feet. In that moment, all I could think about was hoping Claudia was okay, that she made it safely to the rendezvous point, even if I might not. Black spots encroached my vision and then there was nothing.

Armored Hours

Chapter Nine - Marie

Hansen 96

Let's start with the beginning, shall we? My sister, in a past life, fell in love. This was all the way back in the 1600s! It was a swift and unavoidable thing. How she could have fallen for such a brutal monster is beyond me.

She bore him nine children (though three died at an early age) and still felt that wasn't enough, that she needed to do more. Despite his radical political views and preference for military force, she'd witnessed a gentleness in him while he cared for his mother and seven sisters. I think the loss of one of their children as an infant was the tipping point, what drove them both over the edge. Can't really say I blame them for that.

He played it smart in his siege of Drogheda. He had to. His army was in dire need of supplies through the ports, as winter was on its way. I still don't commend him for his actions; they were ruthlessly effective. He just needed one thing to ensure his plan would go smoothly—inside information. And who would be better to retrieve it than my sister? She blended in with the people and didn't raise any suspicions. She could get him the numbers he needed to know.

What they hadn't even considered was what to do if she became ill while undercover. Due to his hold on the town, the citizens and military were unable to leave. Illness and starvation ran rampant, and when he entered the city, his first view was a pile of corpses. One of those corpses was my sister. His rage drove him to massacre instead of siege. While he was busy on his rampage, executing both soldier and civilian, I began the movement of her soul and mine.

He found me mid process of my verbal poetry incanting reincarnation and jumped in… literally. He would not allow me to proceed unless his soul was with hers too. So, what could I do? He had three hooded soldiers with him, and I didn't have the strength to fight against the pain I saw in his eyes. It mirrored my own. Saying the words together felt different and, when we were done, a vibration radiated the air and a prickling sensation ran across my skin.

Of course, I needed to add one more—my beloved. After a long, sincere discussion, he agreed, and we invoked transmigration via hyper focused rumination. I began to feel comfortable with calling for movement of souls through deep thought, but I didn't allow myself to continue. How nice it would have been to bring all of my family members and friends with me. That would have pushed the limits too far. What I had not expected was for it to carry to our child.

Sometimes blessings can be a curse. Though I'm happy to have her with me, she didn't ask for this.

"Do we still have enough flour?" Nelly asks the group, interrupting my memories of the past.

"We've already made enough dough for six loaves. What do we need more flour for?" I ask.

"I don't know how many we're going to have to house nor for how long," Olinda responds with a furrowed brow.

"How long are you keeping the mother and child?" My worry is evident in my tone as I turn to Anna.

"Not sure," she says with a heavy sigh. "Athenaeum could barely get a call through to Southwestern Bell and operator connections. All I know is they're in danger, and I'm protecting them."

"Do you know them at all? Can you trust them?" I inquire, concern lacing my words.

"I know her eldest son," Anna reveals. "His name is Alex, and he takes good care of his sick ma. Actually, he's in Nashville with Claudia and her friends."

"What's he doing with them? He's not part of Athenaeum, is he?" I press for more information.

"No, no, he's there to get me and other customers good whiskey before it's gone."

Anna's statement leaves me momentarily stunned. The mention of alcohol triggers memories of Nelly's reading and her ominous warning: "The first was recently near your blood and the other soon will be."

Is Alex one of the counters I've been desperately searching for? Did Nelly perhaps mean Claudia instead of Anna? Have I been trying to protect the wrong person this whole time? And why would Anna's love go after Claudia?

My mind races with questions as I try to make sense of it all. Where is the other counter? Is one targeting Anna while the other hunts Claudia in order to throw me off their trail? This riddle is becoming increasingly confusing and difficult to decipher. I can't help but wish that Anna had all of my memories so we could work on this together.

"Pass me the salt, please," Olinda requests as she stirs the yeast that's dissolved in water.

Something about watching her stir brings a memory from the future to mind, but what catches me off guard, is that it's not *my* memory. It's Claudia's. This forked path that's been conscripted on us is affecting me more than I anticipated.

The future Claudia is with future Sebastian. My heart clenches at seeing him alive. They're in a small room that I recollect from my memories when I went to another planet to save my daughter. My husband is a scientist in that lifetime and what they're deeply engrossed in can only be described as an experiment. There are bottles of acetone and within the beakers is a milky substance, just like the one Olinda is currently stirring.

A sharp pain shoots through my head as another memory floods my mind. This time, my sister's love stands over her body, lying on a bed for cryogenic freezing. Oh, how I wish we had such advanced technology back in the 1600s. If only I could have saved Anna then, instead of resorting to reincarnation. Perhaps we wouldn't have ended up in this chaotic mess.

But my thoughts quickly shift to the bed next to hers. In this future lifetime, my sister will finally have the child she lost as an infant survive a few years longer. This child appears to be on the verge of a mischievous grin just as the baby had while sleeping. Warmth fills my chest at the thought.

She has such a kind and compassionate heart, wonderful qualities for a parent. I knew he lost them both in this future timeline and it drove him to extremes, conducting scientific experiments that never should come to light. And yet he was able to get away with it for so long because of his position of leadership—a cruel irony in our twisted existence.

Sebastian and I went to severe lengths to control Anna's love during that timeline. I figured he'd just work to reincarnate their child with them. At least, that's what the old memories of the future led me to believe. But something horrible must have changed that I wasn't aware of and now all the memories are beginning to blur for me, causing them to become terribly obscured.

Through the fog of conflicting recollections, a vision emerges. Claudia, summoning telepathy in the future. A powerful ability that changes everything. Was this what forced the break in the fabric? Is this why Anna's love is now after my daughter, hoping to prevent her from shaping the future with her abilities? Even if he succeeds in ending her life in this timeline, she will simply be reincarnated once more.

I struggle to understand it all, but one thing is clear—I need to protect those I care about as much as possible. As I wait for Claudia's return, I make preparations. "I have the materials to make protected charms for everyone staying with us," I announce with a smile.

"It must have cost a fortune to buy so many necklaces," Olinda remarks with a wink.

"Well, I found a more cost-effective method, using rope tied into rings and infused with lavender," I explain.

Nelly offers to cast the protection spell as we assemble the charms.

"Perfect timing," Anna says with relief. "We can work on this while the bread bakes and the dough rises."

Now, I'm seeing the changed or new future timelines flash before me. There's a string connecting the two lines between different worlds, threatening to snap at any minute. But something's different with the additional route.

It's as if Anna and her love are merely ghostly figures, remnants of themselves. As for my family, it's like we take a completely different soul in addition to new bodies and, my breath catches even thinking it, I no longer have memories from the past and the future in this alternate route.

I'm somewhat mollified by the fact that Anna's life continues to get longer with each of the original timelines. I'm grateful her lover was at least considerate of that. But how can I beat him at this game of chess when he seems to be five moves ahead of me at all times?

Everyone can identify a reincarnated soul if they know what to look for; words used at an early age that seem from another time, a preferred style that is classical rather than contemporary, and confessions of déjà vu. It does take a bit of focus but can be done. Our counters have some of these same characteristics, but for those who dabble in spiritual study at all, they usually see a bit of an aura around counters that follows them like a stream.

I'm hoping that these three wonderful women, my friends (and reincarnated sister), by me now can pick up this ability in order to help me. I don't think I'll be able to give them the full story, but close enough to the truth to get them on board. Once I have a team to help me identify who to watch for, it should be easier to track them down and find out what they're up to. I wonder if Anna will protest looking into this Alex for me. And if he's the key to it all.

CHAPTER TEN – CLAUDIA

SWINGING A LAMP
THE CONDUCTOR
ANNOUNCES
"ALL ABOARD,
ALL ABOARD"

Claudia paced back and forth, her heart beating wildly in her chest. The scheduled rendezvous time had long passed, yet there was no sign of Alex. Her throat felt constricted, as if it were covered in velvet, and tears threatened to spill from her eyes. She took a deep breath, trying to calm her nerves. Crying would not bring Alex to her.

Florian tried to ease the tension by suggesting that Alex may just be fashionably late, but Claudia knew this was unlike him.

To make matters worse, his cargo was also nowhere to be seen.

Lina's observation about the missing cargo only added to Claudia's anxiety. Claudia put a fist to her chest and hunched over a bit, a stature of pure agony. Kiersten placed a comforting arm around her, trying to offer solace.

Meanwhile, the Athenaeum men discussed the situation with grave expressions. John suggested checking with a copper, which caused Claudia to gasp. But Michael reassured her that this contact was a friend and could be trusted. Arthur nodded and set out on a mission to check in with the police.

Claudia wrung her hands, feeling torn between hoping they knew where Alex was and dreading the thought that he may have been arrested. Despite the success of their rally and speech, her nerves were frayed. Was all of this worth it if it meant losing someone she had grown deeply attached to?

All of a sudden, the memories came flooding back, and she recalled who had been on the train with them. "What if Kris got to him?" she asked, her voice quivering as she stepped forward.

"Remind me who that is," Florian replied, her interest piqued by the mention of a possible investigative clue. But deep down, she couldn't shake off the feeling of unease that washed over her.

"He was the one at Anna's resort who was rough with a woman there," Lina said hesitantly, a sense of dread clouding her thoughts.

"I hope not," Kiersten added, her face morphed into a concerned expression. "That guy didn't seem to shy away from violence until he was outnumbered."

"He's another bootlegger," Lina mused, her mind racing with possibilities. "And it's no secret that he was jealous of Alex's success."

Claudia continued pacing, her heart still frantically pounding in her chest. She cursed herself for not listening to her instincts and insisting that at least one of the Athenaeum guys accompany Alex. "Where is he?" she asked with desperation, more to herself than anyone else.

Lina caught a glimpse of something in Claudia's eyes, and her own widened in realization. "Wait, are you…" Her words trailed off as she looked at Florian and Kiersten, who seemed strangely unsurprised by the revelation. "Do you care for Alex more than just a friend?"

Claudia let her tears fall freely, her vision blurred as she looked up at Lina and slowly nodded. With her arm now also around Claudia, Lina turned to the others.

"You knew?" She asked Florian and Kiersten, her eyes darting back and forth between them.

"It was easy to see." Kiersten rolled her eyes before placing a hand on Lina's shoulder. "You were too caught up in calculations and navigation plans to notice."

"It's true," Florian chimed in with a mix of fascination and longing. "Their love was blooming right before our very eyes. But you're always so focused on taking care of us to have time to analyze these kind of things."

"I feel like I'm home when I'm with him," Claudia said through sniffles. "And now I feel lost."

Just then, Arthur returned to their group.

"We've received reports of activity at a warehouse known to be frequented by bootleggers," he announced. "But when the police arrived, there was no sign of anyone."

"No bodies?" Kiersten asked hopefully.

Claudia gasped and tried to hold back more tears.

Arthur turned his attention to Claudia. "Do you know if Alex had a meeting scheduled with a Mr. Remus?"

"I know he had a scheduled pick up, but I don't know who from," Claudia managed to say between sobs.

"Based on my read of Alex, I would assume he's the one," Michael said.

"Let's hope they got along," Arthur replied. "The cops say Mr. Remus isn't someone to be messed with."

"Someone followed us here." Florian was trying to figure out how Kris might have interfered.

"Well, if they interrupted a business transaction involving Mr. Remus, I'd say they're the ones in trouble."

Claudia took a deep breath. "So, Alex might be okay?"

"Of course I am, doll," Alex said from behind them. He approached through the crowd, limping as his arm was strung over Adam's shoulders.

"Hey, man, glad you made it." Arthur smiled at Alex.

The girls turned at once in Alex's direction, Claudia a stone statue of shock.

"You're okay?" Claudia stepped toward him, regaining her ability to move. She reached out toward him. "You don't look okay."

"Just a bit bruised up. Nothing that can't heal."

"That's the spirit," Kiersten chimed in.

"I'm sure Claudia can help patch you up," Florian added with a wink.

"What about your cargo?" The ever-vigilant Lina inquired.

"Being secured on the train any minute now," Adam said and nodded at Lina. "Name's Adam."

He extended his hand and, when Lina extended hers, he pressed a kiss to her delicate skin in a very gentlemanly way.

"Looks like love is in the air," Florian stated with a dainty snicker, relieved for Claudia that Alex was okay and taking the moment to ease the tension as Claudia and Alex embraced each other, their bodies shaking with fear and relief.

"That it does," Arthur said while he and Michael watched a group of men in herringbone jackets walk past.

With them was a group of women. The leader wore a monocle. "I wonder if they'll be in our car," Kiersten speculated.

"Or on the steamboat with us," Florian added.

With her friends otherwise occupied, Claudia grabbed Alex's hands and draped his arms over her shoulders. "I was so worried," she whispered to him.

Alex kissed Claudia's forehead. The adrenaline rush had not fully worn off. He thought back to when he woke up. Mr. Remus's men were hauling off Kris's and his companion's unconscious bodies. He'd worried at first that they were dead, but Adam reassured him they weren't. It was one thing to bootleg, but quite another to be involved in murder. So far, he had escaped that sort of lawbreaking.

"You probably need rest," Claudia continued, whispering into his ear.

"Yeah," Alex smiled while replying, but soon his mouth was busy doing something else.

Claudia's lips met Alex's in a fervent kiss, as if it could be their last. The taste of him was intoxicating, overwhelming all her senses. She didn't care that they were out in the open where anyone could see. Her mother's attempts at matchmaking were the least of her concerns now. All she wanted was to be with Alex.

As their lips parted, a dull ache throbbed in Claudia's stomach. A police whistle interrupted their moment, and when they looked up, they saw coppers running toward the cargo area. Without missing a beat, Adam ran after them.

"They're going after our cargo," Adam yelled back to them, pointing at two men in flat caps sprinting towards the train.

Amidst the chaos of people boarding, farewells being said, and luggage being moved by bellhop-hatted attendants, the police became entangled in the fray. Claudia and Alex were both relieved and anxious to have Adam protecting their cargo, but also worried about the growing number of cops around. What if they decided to investigate and discovered what was inside?

Abruptly, the two men in flat caps were closing in on them, headed straight for Claudia and Alex. Without hesitation, Alex tensed his arms around her, his muscles taut against her body. For a brief moment, Claudia panicked and scanned their surroundings for a place to hide. But before she could do anything, she felt the reassuring presence of the Athenaeum men along with her friends flanking their sides, ready to protect them.

A surge of pride filled Claudia's chest as she turned her gaze back to face Kris and his companion, still determinedly making their way through the crowd towards them.

As they approached, Arthur, who had returned just in time, stepped in front of Alex. Claudia didn't fail to notice the switchblade in his hand.

"I just want a word." Kris huffed.

"We can all hear you just fine," Kiersten quipped back. Claudia was pretty sure she also had a knife ready.

"Yeah? Good!" Kris pointed a finger at Alex. "You just couldn't leave things well enough alone. You get all the good booze. It's time for you to let others have their share."

"This is not that time," Adam said, lifting his eyebrows.

"Yeah?" Kris yelled, causing many heads to turn their way, at least the people who had not already noticed the disruption and weren't soaked into the activity at the cargo car. "My guys know where your ma and little brother live. They're going after them if we don't deliver that cargo."

"All aboard, all aboard," the conductor announced.

Kris and his companion sauntered off.

Claudia noticed that Alex was shaking. "We can figure this out and keep them safe," she said to him.

Their group boarded the train, keeping a lookout for Kris the entire time.

Instead of Claudia talking with the conductor, this time Arthur did. He not only secured a seat for Alex next to Claudia, but must have discussed more. Shortly after their conversation, a couple of railroad employees ran past them.

They watched as the two men went to the rear of the car to the cheaper seats outside. After that, they witnessed Kris and his companion being escorted off the train.

"That should slow them down," Arthur said.

"What about my family?" Alex pleaded.

"The conductor is sending a message to the station to be forwarded to your family. He just needs to know where to send it."

"My family doesn't have a phone. Can you send it to Anna Chamberlain at the Chamberlain Resort?"

"Of course, mate."

And with that, he was off to give the directive.

Alex leaned against Claudia, and she placed a comforting hand on his cheek.

"Well, that was a close one," Lina said.

"Glad you guys were with us," Kiersten added, addressing the Athenaeum men.

"Yes, not sure what we would have done without you," Florian closed.

"Thank you," Claudia added.

But instead of verbally responding, Arthur signed *you're welcome*.

John motioned to be quiet and pointed at Alex, who had fallen asleep with his head resting on Claudia's shoulder.

The train fumes filled the car as it began to move. When they left the city, the smell turned to one of fresh air.

Claudia watched her friends silently discuss the rally and following events. She smiled as she felt Alex's breaths get slower and deeper.

As the breeze flew through the car, Claudia was finally able to relax. She rested her head on Alex's and quickly drifted to sleep too. It helped that he was on her hearing side. Placing her good ear against him muted out everything except the ringing, her forever companion of tortured stability.

The dream came to her quickly. It was as if she were in some place in the future. Glass buildings around her reflected the sky, the unending blue gave the impression of being in the middle of the sea. She could hear machines, and they seemed to be everywhere. Something looked different, off really. There wasn't a single living plant within sight.

Then there was a new scene, and Alex was with her. He didn't look like Alex, but she could feel his soul. Cots were lined up all around them as if they were in a hospital wing.

They were in a couple of cots next to one another which had been scooted close. Alex softly brushed his hand up her arm and the particles of her skin exploded with every touch. Her peach fuzz arm hair rose to follow where his hand lead.

The dream quickly shifted and while it was still in the future, it seemed closer to her current time. She saw her mother, not someone who looked like her mother, but with her mother's soul playing the piano on a screen. It was like nothing she'd seen before. The song being played was the wedding march, and when she turned around, she saw Alex.

He again looked different, but she could feel it was him. She was in white, and he was in a tuxedo. He took her hand and then she woke up with a tear of happiness in her eye.

Everyone was exiting the train. Claudia was in a daze from the dreams of other times, and Alex was still recovering from his wounds. Luckily, those traveling with them were organized. Lina made sure their belongings were moved to the steamboat, even Alex's rucksack, which had somehow survived the whole ordeal. The Athenaeum guys were able to confirm the message about Alex's family had been delivered. Anna would be sure they were safe.

"Stay with me," Claudia coaxed Alex. She couldn't stand the thought of being separated. "I have ointment and bandages."

He nodded, and they made their way to Claudia's compartment. Even Lina did not object.

Claudia had one of his arms over her shoulders. Alex had a sadness about him that Claudia wanted to rid. Having slept on the train, they wouldn't be falling asleep quickly. Of course, there are ways to keep worries at bay and Claudia had just the idea.

CHAPTER ELEVEN – ALEX

EYE FOR AN EYE
SHE COST ME MY LOVE
NOW I'M GOING TO TAKE HERS
-DR. CROMWELL'S DIARY

Claudia's request for ice was met with swift action from the kitchen staff, and soon she returned to her quarters on the steamboat with a towel-wrapped bundle in hand. Memories flooded my mind as I watched her work, alone in the dimly lit room. The last time we were here together, our connection had been electric and all-consuming. I shook my head to clear my thoughts and focused on giving Claudia the attention she deserved.

But even as I tried to push away my urges, they came back stronger than ever. That night at the Nichols's Ball, in the cramped storage room where we first met, I couldn't deny my immediate attraction to Claudia. And as I got to know her better, my feelings only grew deeper. Her selflessness in helping Kiersten prepare for the raid, her pure joy at seeing her friends happy at Anna's resort—it all locked me in inexplicably.

As Claudia placed the cold compress on my head, her faint perfume filled my senses, and I couldn't tear my eyes away from hers. The urge to kiss her nearly overwhelmed me, but I knew I couldn't act on it.

I cleared my throat, breaking the intense eye contact. The danger that lurked around me—Kris and his threats toward my family—was a constant reminder of why I couldn't risk getting too close to Claudia. My heart ached at the thought of putting her in harm's way.

But she didn't appear to be at all concerned. With a gentle touch, she placed her hand on my cheek, her fingers cool against my warm skin. "You're going to have a nasty bump if you don't ice this," she remarked, her eyes scanning the visible injury on my head from where the butt of the gun had struck me.

A purple mark was already beginning to form based on my reflection in the mirror. "And why were you limping? What hurts?" She moved her hand down to my leg, searching for any signs of injury with practiced ease. It was clear that she was no stranger to treating wounds and injuries.

"It's just my ankle," I managed to say, but lost the ability to speak when her gentle fingers brushed against my sock. She carefully removed my shoe and rolled off the sock, her touch so soft it caused no additional pain. Then she put a pillow under my foot and moved some of the ice to a different cloth. "Where did you learn first aid?"

Her cheeks flushed a rosy pink as she replied, "Oh, well, Kiersten taught us in preparation for rallies. And my mother's dear friend Olinda runs a shelter where I volunteer, so I've picked up some skills there too."

"A shelter?" I asked, my voice barely a whisper as I tried to comprehend what she was saying.

"Yes," she replied, her tone serious and somber. "It's a safehouse for battered women and their children. A place where they can take refuge and find security."

"It sounds commendable," I said, my voice filled with genuine respect.

"It is," she replied with a hint of pride in her voice. Finally, after placing ice on all of my wounds, she took a seat next to me.

She was silent, staring off, fully at peace or deep in thought. I couldn't tell which. I wanted to know more about her.

"You know, I heard part of your speech earlier," I spoke up, breaking the quiet stillness between us.

Her face lit up with surprise and elation. "You did?"

I nodded, feeling pleased that she was happy to hear it.

"You were so confident and well-spoken," I continued, unable to hide my admiration for her.

She let out a small sigh of relief and twirled a lock of hair between her fingers.

"Do you think it will truly ignite change?" she asked, her eyes flickering with belief juxtaposed by desperation. "I have an upcoming meeting with Frank Newman, Tom

Pendergast, and Walt Disney that I hope will help to move things along."

Without hesitation, I replied, "Definitely!" But a small thought nagged at me. I couldn't help but wonder if there were men who would never support the idea of women being free, no matter how hard women fought. They would try to manipulate and control women, using their own compassion against them. I shuddered at the thought of ever becoming one of those men.

Sadly, these same individuals would use their successful domination over their partners as justification to extend their grasp on others, attempting to force everyone into submission. It was a toxic mindset that destroyed the true beauty of the world around us.

"Can you teach me the secret language that you and your friends use to communicate silently?" I asked Claudia, eager to learn more about their unique way of communication.

She raised an eyebrow in surprise before answering, "You want to learn sign language?"

I nodded eagerly, finally understanding the subtle yet powerful form of communication they used amongst themselves.

"With my unilateral deafness, I picked it up. I suffered a serious ear infection in my hearing ear a couple years back and could not hear a thing. Lina had already picked up a few things and taught Kiersten and Florian. They're fluent now. It's really remarkable."

"You have smart friends. Of course, they'd continue to communicate with you."

She smiled warmly and replied, "Let's start with the alphabet. Some words have to be fingerspelled, so it's a good base."

We went through the letters one by one, with Claudia patiently correcting my handshapes and movements. She even taught me a fun game where she would spell out a three-letter word and then I had to use the last letter to spell a new word. Apparently, a local teacher by the name of Kerns had shown her the game.

As we continued practicing, Claudia yawned, and her head slowly lowered onto the side pillow. Her long hair cascaded in all directions, but I gently brushed it back with my fingers so that I wouldn't accidentally lie on it.

Her hair was incredibly soft and voluminous, framing her face like a halo. With her features relaxed in sleep, her smooth skin resembled polished marble. As her lips parted slightly, I watched as she drifted off into a peaceful slumber.

I watched over her as she lay unconscious. The gentle rise and fall of her chest filled my heart with love, and I couldn't help but feel a sense of protectiveness towards her.

She deserved the best of everything, yet here I was, putting her in danger.

As the sun began to rise, its warm rays danced across the water around the boat, illuminating Claudia's room through the small window. I couldn't tear my eyes away from her sleeping form, still lost in thoughts of how to protect her.

Back in Kansas City, we disembarked from the boat. The Athenaeum men bid us farewell and went their separate ways. Michael whispered in Kiersten's ear before leaving. While I was interested to learn what was said, my worry for my family overshadowed that. My own team of Thomas, James, and Frank were there to greet us and collect the cargo, ready to move it to a secure location. I breathed a sigh of relief at having them there with us.

"What happened to you?" Thomas asked with concern as he inspected the gnarly bruise on my forehead.

"Kris is after our cargo, and he tried to take it from me," I replied grimly, pointing to my injury. "He hit me with his gun."

"Why I ought to…" James fumed, his fists clenched tightly.

"They're going after my ma and little brother," I explained urgently. "Can you handle things here while I make sure they're safe?" My words were rushed as panic started to set in at the thought of my family being in danger.

"Of course," said Frank with a confident nod. "Shall we meet you once we're finished?"

My heart swelled with gratitude for my reliable friends. "Not yet," I responded quietly, grateful for their understanding. "I don't want to draw attention to their whereabouts."

Claudia's eyes widened in understanding, and she spoke in a hushed tone, "Would your family have gone into hiding after receiving your message?"

"Yes, I know exactly where they'd go." As I stood away from the group, I made a subtle gesture with my hand: fist for the letter A in front of my chest, first two fingers over thumb for the letter N, lifting and lowering them for another N, and finally forming the letter A again. Anna.

"Want us to come with you?" Kiersten asked as she approached, her concern evident on her face.

"We're trying to be inconspicuous," Claudia said to her gently.

"Rendezvous later?" Florian chimed in, joining Kiersten with a worried smile in her eyes.

"At the attic?" Claudia inquired about their meeting location.

Lina nodded confidently in agreement. "We need to discuss the recent clinic raids." Claudia's eyebrows raised, and I had a sneaking suspicion that must have been what the Athenaeum man whispered to Kiersten, who then informed Lina.

"You should go with them," I urged Claudia, wanting to protect her from any potential danger.

"I think we should move your family from Anna's place to Olinda's safehouse," Claudia whispered, leaning in so that only I could hear. "There won't be as much foot traffic there. And I can personally vouch for them."

I gave in and as we drove to Anna's together, I couldn't help but feel giddy about Claudia meeting my family. That's probably the opposite of how I should have been feeling, as I wanted to protect her, but the emotion was undeniable.

"How old is your brother?" Claudia's innocent question broke through my thoughts, and I couldn't help but smile at her curiosity.

"Wendell is twelve. He's quite unique, always studying how people think and function."

"That sounds fascinating. And what about your ma?"

I could see the worry in Claudia's fidgeting hands.

"My ma will adore you, don't worry."

Her smile lit up the entire car, easing some of my fears.

I parked as close as possible, not wanting Claudia to walk alone, even for a few steps.

"Welcome, welcome, my dears," Anna greeted us warmly with a hug for Claudia and a handshake for me.

"Where can we find my ma and brother?"

"They're in room ten."

"Thank you for housing them during this emergency," Claudia said to Anna.

"Of course," Anna responded. "I greatly appreciate how Alex cares for his family, and I'm happy to help."

"Would you horribly mind if we moved them to Olinda's?"

"Of course not."

Despite the sharp pain shooting through my ankle, I pushed myself to move faster. Claudia and Anna followed me at a slower pace. I overheard them talking, but didn't slow down to hear the entire conversation. I found the door to be locked when I tried the knob, which was probably good. The tension to see they were okay was almost unbearable.

"Ma, it's me," I called out.

There was some shuffling about, and then I heard the door unlock.

"Alex," Ma said when she opened the door. She had me in a bearhug before I could make sure Wendell was okay.

Then she gently pushed me back, inspecting my face, concern etched in her features. "What happened to you?"

"Nothing I can't handle, Ma." Anna and Claudia had caught up by then. "Actually, Claudia here nursed my wounds. They'd be even worse without her ice."

As my ma's eyes widened in surprise, she enveloped Claudia in a warm hug. Claudia initially tensed but then relaxed and returned the embrace with a genuine smile.

"Wh...Who...who's that?" I turned to Wendell.

Claudia, free from my ma now, said, "I'm Claudia. It's a pleasure to meet you." She extended her hand for a shake.

Stuttering even more now, Wendell managed to get out, "I...It...It's a pl...pleasure to m...meet you too."

Wendell's face turned as red as a tomato.

"Ah, she doesn't care about your stutter." I placed a hand on my brother's shoulder. "She asked about you on the way over and would like to get to know you."

Wendell looked up at Claudia with curious eyes, intrigued by this new person, who seemed genuinely interested in him.

"Did you know that I have a deaf ear?" Claudia asked, pushing her hair behind that ear to show him the culprit. "And sometimes I have infections in this one." She showed the other ear. "My friends have actually learned sign language so we can communicate with our hands when I struggle to hear."

Ma watched them converse with adoration. As Wendell discussed his studies on stutters, I asked Ma, "Would you be all right if we moved you to a safehouse with less traffic?"

"Anna has been a marvelous host, but if it's what you think is best." She shrugged.

Claudia and I helped Ma and Wendell pack, which didn't take long as they packed the bare necessities in the sudden move.

The winding drive to Olinda's was filled with chatter as Claudia excitedly shared all the good work that their host does.

"I'm Dorothy, by the way," Ma said to Claudia. "Thank you for caring after my family."

"Well, Dorothy, you probably shouldn't thank me yet. Olinda could use some help, so she'll more than likely put you to work."

I gave Claudia a worried look, hoping she remembered that my ma was not in the best of health. She put a hand on my arm in reassurance, silently understanding.

"Don't mind that a bit. I'll be glad to be of some use."

They both smiled.

At the door, Olinda greeted them with open arms. The house was spacious, but it had a warmth and coziness that made it feel like home—a stark contrast to the elegant mirrors and chandeliers at Anna's. Ma took a deep breath and seemed to relax even more, the smell of fresh bread filling her senses.

Olinda handed all of us rings made of rope. As she discussed their importance, Claudia and Ma put them on their fingers. Wendell raised a brow, and I did too. I put my ring in my trouser pocket and Wendell followed suit.

It was a relief to have my family settled in. We hugged goodbye. As much as I disliked leaving them, I needed to secure the shipment and find Kris.

Once Claudia and I exited Olinda's, I said, "Well, I need to be off to help my team move our product."

"You should call the Athenaeum gentlemen to help you," Claudia offered as we walked to the car. "Could expedite the process."

"Yeah, I'll think about it."

She curled her lower lip in a pout as we got into the car.

"Don't you find it a little convenient that Kris knew exactly where I was going at the same time as their joining our group?" I asked, while starting the engine and driving.

She let out an exasperated breath.

"Even you had an ominous feeling when they first appeared."

"Well then, let me and the girls help."

I was silent, mulling over what to say next. The look of admonishment she gave me let me know I'd made an error.

"You don't think women can handle hard labor. I'll have you know…"

"No, no. That's not it."

I let out a frustrated sigh.

"Don't you need to meet?" I floundered. "Lina said something about clinic raids."

She folded her arms across her chest and remained silent for a torturous amount of time.

"I can drop you off. It's on the way."

"Thank you," she said curtly. "Actually, I'll take this." She removed the tie she'd gifted me, the material rubbed against my neck. "You can have it back the next time I see you."

As I drove up, my heart was in turmoil. Part of me wanted to fix things between us, to hold Claudia close and apologize for causing her pain. But another part of me knew that it was best for her to stay away from me, at least until the danger passed. Her tear-filled eyes and the slamming of the car door only added to my inner conflict. As I watched her retreat inside, I couldn't help but wonder if I had ruined any chance of a future with the woman of my dreams.

Armored Hours

Chapter Twelve - Marie

Hansen 132

Armored Hours

My house is not quiet this evening. Unexpected visitors arrived in a flurry. Something about their evening being interrupted, and they just needed a place to meet in peace. They wouldn't be a bother.

The comforting chatter of Claudia and her friends fills my den, the warmth of their presence seeping into every corner. The flickering fire casts a soft glow on their faces as they huddle together, seeking solace in each other's company. I catch snippets of their conversation as I prepare tea in the kitchen, grateful to finally be in the loop.

Claudia's voice carries a hint of worry as she confides in her friends about the police officer who has been harassing Kiersten's workplace. It saddens me that even in this safe space, they're unable to meet without fear or interruption. But at least they have each other for support.

As I listen to them talk, I can't help but feel grateful for their lively presence in my home. They breathe life into it, filling it with laughter and strength. And although Claudia may not confide in me, I'm glad she has a strong support system in her friends. Despite my years of experience, I know that sometimes all we need is someone who understands and supports us.

"I keep getting word of more and more raids," I overhear Kiersten say.

"What, and they're not being reported in the papers?" Claudia's friend, Lina, is full of sarcasm. "Thank you for keeping me in the loop, by the way."

"We should just hide birth control in garments at dress shops," this must be from Florian. "The men would never catch on."

"How much damage has there been?" I can hear the concern in Claudia's voice.

"Most clinics have fared well enough, but there's a dire shortage of birth control," Lina says.

"Of course they'd go after that," Kiersten scoffs. "Gotta keep their wives pregnant and confined to the home."

"Is it truly so difficult for men to understand how to please a woman?" Florian has a point.

"I've received word from overseas, thanks to Kiersten's intel," Lina adds. "There's a shipment coming in soon. I've meticulously planned out the logistics."

"But what about the meeting to secure freedom for women in Kansas City?" Claudia interjects.

"You must tell me everything about your meeting with Frank Newman, Tom Pendergast, and Walt Disney." The air was knocked out of me at the mention of those names by Florian.

Claudia was certainly in over her head. Frank Newman is the premier exhibitor in Kansas City. If a counter connects with him or if he is a counter himself, he could easily get a message out to the masses. The potential consequences and disruption this could bring upon the timeline are unimaginable.

"Yes, I would love to work at one of his shows," Kiersten adds excitedly. "I could retire off the tips I'd make."

Tom Pendergast, once an alderman, now held sway over local politics with ease. His close ties to the Irish community were likely how Claudia made her connection.

The connection between Newman and Disney was unmistakable, like a thread connecting two distant worlds. I have a future memory of the animated cartoon laugh-o-grams to be aired. But what could Claudia hope to gain, meeting with the three men? What was her motive?

"We should make it back in time for your meeting," Lina reports. "We'll need to return to St. Louis first and then Bessie will fly us to Boston."

"Can Bessie spend time with us?" Kiersten asks. "She's simply fabulous."

"No, unfortunately, she cannot," Lina answers. "She has other obligations that require her presence in Paris."

Florian lets out a disappointed sigh. "That's a shame. It would be lovely to spend some time with her, even if only briefly."

"Is there no way to expedite the trip?" Claudia inquires.

"Hm, perhaps Bessie could intercept the ship during its route instead of when it leaves." I wasn't sure how Lina thought they could do this. She must know more about flying and Bessie's abilities than I. It was as if I could hear Lina's internal calculations out loud. "Yes, maybe she could link up with the ship on the way to Paris."

Kiersten jumps in excitedly. "Then maybe we could spend more time with her!" Her fondness for Bessie Coleman is evident in every word she utters.

"Then it's settled," Florian says. "When do we leave for St. Louis?"

"The day after tomorrow."

With that, the girls bid each other farewell, and I finally have some time alone with my daughter at last.

The setting sun casts a warm orange glow over the room as I invite Claudia to join me for a cup of tea. But as she walks in, I notice the tears in her eyes from before are back. I had hoped her friends would rid her of the sadness, but now I see that her eyes are red from crying. She saved them for once her friends had left.

"What is troubling you, my dear?" I ask gently.

Claudia hesitates before finally opening up to me. "Has a man ever distanced himself from you? Someone you were interested in?"

"You're interested in a man?"

"Mother! Please set aside your inclination to take charge of my courtships for one evening," Claudia pleads, frustrated with my tendency to meddle.

"What makes you think this man, whoever he is, wants distance?"

"Alex just seemed to push for me to focus on the girls instead of helping him."

"Is this the Alex who was on the trip with you?"

"Yes, he was such a dream during our travels…"

As Claudia continues on about the details of her relationship with Alex, I can't shake the feeling of him possibly being a counter. If Claudia doesn't reincarnate going forward, it would eliminate whatever happened to instigate my sister's love's vengeance. She'd be more likely to live a content and happy life in this timeline. Would she be fulfilled with that?

"There, there, everything will be all right," I say to my daughter. "Here, take a few more of these rings for your friends and keep them with you for protection."

"How do you know everything will be all right?"

"I just do."

"Thank you for the rings, I guess."

Claudia looks at me, her eyes full of questions. It's true in this timeline I've lived a pretty privileged life, but she doesn't know of the other lives I've lived. Then she looks at a photo of myself and her late father. I'm smiling at him in a way only reserved for true love and unbridled joy.

I pour my sweet child more tea.

"Can I tell you something?" she asks, her voice barely above a whisper. My breath catches in my throat as I wait for her to continue. This is what I've been waiting for. For so long I've wished she would confide in me like this. And yet, now that she finally is, I find myself filled with reservations.

"Anything." It is the only answer I can give her. A mother's love truly knows no bounds.

"Lately I've been having dreams from other times."

I nearly choke on my tea. This is concerning news indeed. Maybe I'm paranoid. They are just dreams, after all.

"Like when you were a child? Dreams from back then?" I try to rationalize.

"No." She shakes her head, her hand trembling as she sets down her teacup. "Like different lifetimes. Alex is with me in the ones from the future."

Well, that definitely changes things. Every part of my being wants to ask her for more details. What if I could stop something bad from happening in the future? If she and I could work as a team, perhaps we'd stand against the duplicate counters. No, I can't chance it. She's head over heels for this Alex guy. Isn't his future appearance in her dreams a clear sign that he is one of the counters?

"You know, sometimes absence makes the heart grow fonder."

She huffs in exasperation. "Even after I told you, you're still on this ridiculous, most eligible bachelor hunt."

"Dear," I plead, trying to calm her down.

"Well, don't worry about it." She sighs heavily and throws her hands in the air. "The girls and I are going on a trip without him, so both of you can have the distance you crave."

"That's not what I meant," I say, feeling defeated.

"Good night, Mother." She stomps out of the kitchen. Whatever connection we'd made in that moment was severed as quickly as it had come on.

"Good night," I call after her softly, my heart heavy with disappointment. Perhaps it's for the best. Tonight is another full moon cycle, and I need to meet my friends. There's serious business to attend to tonight.

The silver beams of the full moon dance across the rippling surface of the pond, casting a mystical glow upon our meeting spot. The ancient trees surrounding us cast long shadows that seem to stretch towards us like grasping fingers.

We exchange our usual greetings—hugs and smiles and excited chatter. How I do love having Anna here with us again. But tonight, there is a sense of urgency in my bones, and I cut straight to the chase, as I always do.

"Ladies," I begin, my voice carrying over the gentle rustling of leaves and chirping of crickets, "you're all familiar with incantations. But have any of you heard of the one for reincarnation?"

I know that I'm risking adding more people to the already crowded reincarnation pool—Olinda and Nelly, to be exact. But I can't let fear hold me back. Whatever hiccups this may cause, I'll have to face them head on. Besides, if my enemy is going to have his own help throughout space and time, it's only fair that I do too.

"What on earth are you talking about?" Nelly asks, her brows furrowed in confusion. I had hoped she would be the first to understand, with her fortune-telling abilities. But perhaps she's upset for not foreseeing this.

"I did not originate from this time," I explain, my voice low and mysterious. "I come from a much more distant past."

A hush falls over our group as they process this information, a look of shock plastered on their faces.

"I've always thought your style was classical," Olinda remarks, breaking the silence. She tilts her head in contemplation.

"That is one way to spot a reincarnated soul," I reply with a slight smile. It's fascinating how different people can have glimpses of their past lives in small ways.

"What are the others?" Anna pipes up, her curiosity piqued. I can tell she's noticed some similarities between herself and me.

"Often people will use words from another time at an early age," I continue, "and they also experience déjà vu." Anna's eyes light up with recognition, but she looks at the others and holds back from saying anything else.

"I am an anomaly," I declare boldly. "I carry all memories from before, whereas most people only have a vague sense of having lived before. And for many, that feeling fades after childhood."

My companions stare at me in awe, unable to comprehend such a concept. Even Anna's usually composed expression mirrors their shock.

"But it doesn't stop there," I reveal. "I also have memories of my future lives."

Nelly's eyes widen in excitement. "So do you know of future inventions?" she asks eagerly, unable to contain her curiosity.

I nod.

"And remedies?" Olinda asks, the inquisitiveness spreading.

I nod again, this time in response to Olinda's question about remedies, feeling overwhelmed with the weight of my knowledge. Anna notices and empathetically adds her own comment.

"That must be incredibly confusing," she says, her voice full of concern.

I can't disclose too much, so I simply nod again.

"My foe has done something despicable in the future," I finally confess. "He's spawned back twice over for vengeance and is after Claudia."

Anna's selfless nature shines through as she immediately asks, "How can we help?" But I am torn—my true motive is to protect Anna, but I cannot say that aloud in front of her, possibly altering her timeline.

"Those who reincarnate for ulterior motives share certain characteristics like classic style and speaking," I explain. "They also emit a faint aura that follows them, leaving a trail behind. If we cast a revealing spell, we may be able to identify them."

Olinda asks how to cast the spell, while Nelly expresses concern about having to search through everyone in town.

She asks if they are in town at all, or if we will have to travel far.

"They're definitely in town," I assure them with a sigh. The thought of possibly having to search beyond our small town makes my stomach churn with unease.

And so I tell them about the spell, my heart racing as I reveal my desperate plan. Olinda's dark eyes widen in disbelief, her long fingers nervously tapping against the sides of her thighs. But after a moment of hesitation, she nods and agrees to keep an eye on Alex when he visits his family. I can see the doubt in her expression, but she trusts me enough to go along with it.

Next, I turn to Anna, feeling guilty for dragging her into this mess. She looks at me with concern etched in her features as I explain that I need her to watch Vernon—the man who has been harassing the girls at Kiersten's workplace. Despite her reservations, she swears to help in any way she can. I know he visits her establishment, so it makes sense that she tackles this one, but that doesn't make me feel better about it. Hopefully, he'll at least abide by the law.

Lastly, I turn to Nelly, knowing that what I'm about to ask may be crossing a line. But desperate times call for desperate measures. I need Kris to procure alcohol for a charity gala that Nelly is hosting, so she can also identify whether he is a counter or not. He was involved in going after Alex's family, and I have a feeling he may be connected to other nefarious activities as well. It needs to be done but the thought of putting Nelly in harm's way weighs heavily on my mind.

As the meeting draws to a close, I feel a mix of relief and guilt wash over me. I know I've asked a lot from my friends and there's no telling what consequences may come from involving them in this dangerous game. At least now I don't have to face it alone.

CHAPTER THIRTEEN – CLAUDIA

HAVING FULFILLED ALL THE CONDITIONS
REQUIRED
BY THE Fédération Aéronautique Internationale,
FOR AN AVIATOR PILOT
IS HEREBY BREVETTED AS SUCH

The girls nestled closely together on a worn, creaky wooden bench at the bustling train station. Their eyes darted back and forth, scanning the crowds for their friend's familiar face. Lina's gaze lingered on the ornate clock that adorned the wall, its hands ticking away the seconds with precision. She couldn't help but admire the delicate etchings and engravings that adorned its surface, a testament to the craftsmanship. Kiersten's eyes lit up as she spotted Bessie, and she ran towards her with arms outstretched. The pilot seemed overwhelmed by the attention but welcomed Kiersten's hug with a warm smile.

"Simmer down, Kiersten." Florian chuckled as she approached and gave Bessie a side hug.

Lina shook Bessie's hand with enthusiasm. "It's so great to see you. My friends and I have been on back-to-back trips."

Claudia joined in, waving to Bessie as she approached. "We're not used to traveling so frequently. I don't know how you do it."

Bessie shrugged modestly. "Well, for starters, my trips are usually a lot less crowded." She smiled at them all. "Shall we head to my place?"

"We're not going directly to the plane?" Lina's brow furrowed in confusion, wanting to stick to her strict schedule.

"No, haven't you heard?" Bessie asked with a hint of mystery.

Claudia and her friends exchanged puzzled glances, none of them aware of what Bessie could be referring to.

As Bessie drove them to her place, she filled them in on the change of plans. Her trip to Europe was put on hold due to conflict with suffragettes overseas who disapproved of the American movement's treatment of advocates based on race. As a result, she needed to attend urgent meetings at the YWCA. She also informed them that the shipment of birth control they were after had been delayed as well. It seemed their entire trip would have to be postponed as they redirected their efforts towards this essential cause.

Lina's determination to help all women gain more rights outweighed her dislike for changing plans. Kiersten and Florian shared this understanding, knowing that the fight for women's suffrage in America would not reach everyone. Some Native Americans, Puerto Ricans, and black women would still be left without the right to vote. And as women who loved other women, they recognized their own need to continue fighting for equal rights.

Claudia, on the other hand, knew just how close she'd be to losing her right to vote if the new laws didn't include everyone. If her non-deaf eardrum ruptured, and she was unable to confirm her identity at the election poll, to answer all the verbal questions correctly, she'd lose the right to vote as well. She dove in wholeheartedly, going to the YWCA with Bessie even when the others didn't. Missing the meeting back home was a small sacrifice to make for such an important cause, and she didn't mind her mother taking her place through letters.

The girls anxiously fretted over Bessie's impending weekly rate increase, fearing that their extended stay with her would add to the already hefty bill. As a frequent traveler, Bessie had chosen a residential hotel in St. Louis over a more burdensome living situation that would require constant upkeep. The building's uniform brick exterior stood in stark contrast to the opulent and vibrant interior, adorned with intricate crown molding and polished porcelain floors. Claudia vividly recalled the satisfying click of their heels as they made their way through the grand lobby. Despite their demanding work schedules, they always made time to indulge in the smooth melodies of jazz bands at the nearby dance hall.

As time passed, months flew by, and they found themselves sending letters home to explain their extended stay in St. Louis. Lina rejoiced at the news of a new shipment of birth control, and they made haste to ensure its retrieval. Bessie's determination to make it to Paris only grew stronger, as there were important people she needed to meet. More letters were sent home with an updated return date, as their dedication to the fight for women's rights never wavered.

Bounding through the open field, the girls were bombarded with a swirling dust cloud kicked up by the powerful propellers of their aircraft. Bessie provided fleece-lined boots and jackets. Take off was so loud it almost drowned out Claudia's ninety decibel tinnitus. With anticipation building, the girls peered out the window as the ground beneath them rushed by in a blur, until suddenly they were lifted into the air and soaring above the landscape. Florian's grip on Claudia's arm tightened as the rush of flying caused her heart to race. She had never experienced anything like it before.

"This is incredible!" Kiersten exclaimed with glee.

"Easy for you to say," Florian replied, looking pale and queasy.

"Just wait until we level out," Bessie reassured them. "Then we'll be flying amongst the clouds!"

Claudia fell silent as she took in the breathtaking view below, buildings shrinking into tiny specks and fluffy clouds hovering beside them.

"As discussed, this plane can also land on water," Bessie reminded them. "I've already coordinated with Captain Hansen and will radio ahead. Then I get to have fun aerial refueling."

"And then a smaller boat will come to collect us," Lina added. "Good thing I advised everyone to pack light."

Florian let out an anxious sigh. "That doesn't sound simple at all."

"We'll manage," Kiersten encouraged.

"We're all in this together," Claudia added determinedly. "Bessie, is aerial refueling safe?"

"I'm not afraid of it," Bessie said. "Many pilots do it in order to set new distance records."

They all took deep breaths as Bessie expertly landed the plane on the choppy Atlantic water. The waves reached up toward the majestic clouds in the sky as the sun shone through. As the plane rocked with the water, Claudia feared it could be in danger of tipping over.

Lina swung open the door and yelled for the crew on the forty-five-foot boat. Gripping tightly onto the plane handle, she stepped out and watched as a crew member grabbed her bag and tossed it onto the boat. With a strong hand, he hoisted Lina into the bobbing boat, readying to guide them to their next destination.

"Catch," Kiersten yelled before tossing him her bag. Thankfully, he laughed, enjoying her spirit, and caught the bag with ease. She was very lithe, maneuvering into the boat.

Florian daintily stepped down but froze in fear and was unable to hand her bag over, let alone move herself to the boat. Claudia rushed to her side.

"You can do this," Claudia assured Florian. "Here, let me take your bag." She was able to hand the bag over.

"You guys can handle this without me," Florian told the girls. "I'll just go with Bessie to Paris. I've always wanted to go to Paris."

"One problem," Bessie yelled. "You just handed over your passport."

"Look, he's very strong." Claudia pointed to the man on the boat, who then flexed his muscles.

Florian took a deep breath and finally reached out. Everyone cheered once she was aboard. As Claudia pondered how difficult it would be to move Florian to the larger ship, she noticed a large wave headed in their direction.

"Hold tight to the boat," she yelled at her friends.

She held her breath, watching. The boat rocked violently, but did not tip over or throw anyone out. The relief was short-lived though, as the wave wasn't done. In fact, it had only been building. When it crashed into the plane, Claudia felt her legs swept off the step and then the force wrenched her hand from the handle.

The water rushed up and sucked her under. The combination of her spinning body and altered balance from her deaf ear made it impossible to tell which direction she was going. Terror clogged her throat and stuttered her heart. More water rushed past her as she sunk; it was absolute panic and chaos. She thought for one brief moment: *perhaps now I'll be with father.*

Hooks clamped her arms under her armpits, stopping her from drowning.

A boat crew member had dove in and his arms were under hers, lifting her to the surface. Claudia gratefully gulped air when they rose above the water. He lifted her up with a determined look on his face and another crew member hoisted her into the boat. Her friends gathered around, but the crew requested space to wrap a blanket around her and to check her pulse and breathing.

Despite the shock of what had just happened, Claudia and her friends all watched Bessie take off, grateful the plane had not been capsized with the horrific wave.

As they neared the almost four hundred feet freighter with a triple expanse steam engine, Claudia's teeth chattered uncontrollably from the cold. The girls marveled at the size of the ship as they approached. It towered over them, tall in some areas and shorter in others, where a massive crane was stationed. At least, that's what Lina thought it was.

As they drew closer, some of the crew lowered a sturdy ladder for them to climb up. Claudia's muscles were strained and weak from her struggle in the water, but she managed to pull herself up with determination. The man who had saved her approached them.

"You must get her into dry clothes immediately," he instructed Lina with a sense of urgency.

The other man chimed in, "I'll show you to your room."

They made their way from the deck, down a steep flight of stairs, and through a narrow hallway until they reached a door that led to their living quarters on the ship. Despite everything that had happened, Claudia couldn't help but be fascinated by the inner workings of the massive freighter.

"We have one room with two bunks for you." He opened the door, and the girls filtered in except for Kiersten, who remained in the hall.

"Can you show me to the kitchen?" she asked, her voice laced with concern. "I need to make my friend some hot tea."

"Right this way."

Florian and Lina helped Claudia into some dry clothes. They had to lend her some of theirs as her bag was lost to the sea.

Kiersten returned with a steaming mug in hand but wore a worried expression on her face. "You guys...I think I saw Vernon on the way back," she said grimly. "I'm glad I brought my knives."

Claudia took a sip of the fragrant tea, holding onto the mug for warmth. "Vernon? The cop who busted our meeting place?"

"Yes," Kiersten confirmed. She then asked, "Does he have access to the attic? Could he have seen our plans?"

"But why would he follow us?" Florian interjected. "Our plans have changed. Even if he did see our original ones, he wouldn't know about our new ones."

"Our contact overseas knew about our updated plans," Claudia added. "Their name was on the paperwork."

"But they're risking their own safety by collaborating with us," Kiersten argued. "Why would they share that information?"

"Perhaps they were captured by their authorities," Claudia suggested with a frown. "They may have given up information in exchange for a more lenient sentence."

"How the hell are we supposed to secure and transport this product with the damn police on board?" Kiersten exclaimed, her brow furrowed in frustration.

"We'll have to enlist the help of the crew," she continued. "They seem decent enough, at least the ones who helped us get on board and the kitchen staff."

Florian let out a tired sigh. "That's a good idea, but I don't know about you guys, I'm exhausted."

Lina nodded in agreement. "I think Claudia could use some rest too after nearly drowning."

"I'll take first watch," Kiersten stated firmly, determination glinting in her eyes.

As they took turns keeping watch through the night, Claudia tossed and turned in fitful sleep. Her dreams were plagued by visions of other times, growing more vivid and frequent with each passing day. She couldn't shake off the feeling that something was coming, something big.

A sharp knock on their door interrupted their restless slumber. "Chow will be ready in twenty minutes," a crew member announced.

Kiersten opened the door, her eyes scanning the hallway for any signs of danger. "Can I help out in the kitchen?" she asked, trying to keep her voice steady.

The crew member shrugged nonchalantly. "I don't see why not. I'm sure they could use an extra hand."

Kiersten ducked her head back in before leaving. "I'll see if I can get any information on Vernon and what he's doing here."

"And we'll secure our goods." Lina waved goodbye.

"Won't it be dangerous to hold them the entire trip?" Kiersten asked. "Should we wait until we're closer to Boston?"

"Should have asked Bessie to wait for us, get what we came after, and left," Florian said as she sneered at the blanket while making her bunk for the day.

"She needs to get to Europe and learn how the suffragettes there include all races in their fight to try to fix the gaping holes left by the Nineteenth Amendment," Claudia said, her voice a little louder than usual.

"Don't worry," Lina insisted. "Everything will get sorted."

They made their way to the dining area. Claudia and Florian separated from Lina, who headed towards the cargo bay, while they continued on towards the kitchen.

As they walked, a melodic tune drifted down the hallway. They couldn't help but smile when they saw Kiersten singing "Anchors Away" with the staff in the kitchen.

"She always makes friends so quickly," Florian said, and Claudia gave her a side hug. Despite not always agreeing, Claudia didn't know what she'd do without her friends.

Florian and Claudia settled into their seats, slowly savoring their meals as they scanned the dining hall for signs of Vernon. Lina and Kiersten soon joined them, updating them on their plans.

"I stashed our package in the cargo bay," Lina stated. "The workers there are sympathetic to our cause and will keep an eye out for any suspicious activity."

"The kitchen staff is also on our side," Kiersten chimed in. "They're not big fans of the authorities who may be after us."

"So what do we do now?" Florian asked. "We can't just wait around like sitting ducks."

"We run an investigation of our own," Claudia answered. "Did the kitchen staff have to deliver Vernon's breakfast to his room? I haven't noticed him here."

"Let me check." With that, Kiersten leapt up and raced back to the kitchen.

Lina's eyes widened in shock. "You want us to spy on him?"

"We have to know his plan," Claudia replied with determination.

"Too bad I left my perfect incognito outfit at home." Florian rubbed her temples in frustration.

"We'll just have to improvise," Lina said, a hint of intensity in her voice. "We can grab some clothes from the crew's laundry on our way."

"Sorry for the delay. Helped with the dishes while gathering information. I have his room number and, yes, he's having breakfast in his room."

"What are we waiting for?" Claudia was ready to set out on this mission. She was tired of Vernon interfering.

They made their way to the laundry and grabbed jackets and hats. Luckily, they had dawned overalls. If their choice of wear had been skirts, it would have easily given them away.

As they crept down the hallway towards Vernon's room, Claudia's heart pounded with nerves and anticipation. She was done playing by his rules. Standing outside his room, they heard voices.

"We have to wait until they have the contraband in hand to make the arrest," Vernon said to someone. "Now, get back to surveillance. I'll have your job if you fail."

As the doorknob turned, the girls walked as quickly but nonchalantly as they could down the hall. Before making it five steps, they heard a voice.

"Hey," a man yelled out at them.

"Freeze," Vernon screamed as he exited his room.

The girls froze, and Kiersten retrieved a knife from her pocket.

"Turn around slowly," Vernon instructed.

As they turned, Claudia noticed two things: Vernon's loaded gun aimed in their direction, and Kiersten raising her knife. Claudia's adrenaline spiked so quickly she almost became dizzy. Fear pulsed through her veins as she screamed, "No!" and desperately lunged two steps toward Vernon.

Everything blipped. The lights flickered, and the ship tilted, throwing everyone against the wall. Ship alarms blared all around them. In that moment, Claudia knew something had gone terribly wrong.

CHAPTER FOURTEEN – ALEX

THE FIRST LINE OF THIS TELEGRAM CONTAINS
THE FOLLOWING PARTICULARS IN ORDER NAMED
PREFIX LETTERS AND NUMBER OF MESSAGE
OFFICE ORIGIN, NUMBER OF WORDS, DATE
TIME HANDED IN AND OFFICIAL INSTRUCTIONS

I thought I was doing the right thing by putting distance between me and Claudia. I wanted to protect her, but now it feels like a terrible decision. Her letter arrived months ago, telling me their trip had been delayed. But then the news came in that their entire ship had vanished without a trace. Her mother organized a search party to find her, but Kris appeared with the tie Claudia gifted me and then kept for herself.

He'd evaded me, darn him. He had a friend just around the corner. Was he taunting me? We'd kept my family safe from him thus far and delivered our inventory to customers.

"My uncle says the S.S. Hewitt made her regular calls and didn't report anything unusual only days before going missing," James said, interrupting my thoughts.

"I don't understand how Kris would have the tie," Frank added. "He's here, and she's hundreds of miles away."

"At least she has her friends with her," Thomas said, reading the concern on my face.

Wanting to keep her safe might have put her in the most danger of all. What had I done?

We were gathered at Kiersten's workplace, and I couldn't help but think back to the notes I'd seen in the attic while moving the booze. I desperately wanted to go back up there and see if there were any clues that could help us find Claudia.

"Let's hope none of this has anything to do with the reported explosion or piracy," James said grimly.

"Not helping," I pleaded.

"Could Kris have connections secretly planning to take the ship and use it wholly as a rum runner?" Frank questioned.

"They do charge an arm and a leg to rent space on a bonified cargo ship," Thomas seemed to think the potential for Kris to steal the ship was plausible.

"He couldn't tackle something that large, and you know it," I rejected the thought.

We all took a drink and sat in silence for a while. They knew I was upset, but they didn't know that I was completely falling apart inside. Claudia and I had grown so close during the months we spent together before she left. In a perfect world, we could have been courting each other without constantly being in danger.

If only I didn't have to bootleg in order to support my family after my da passed, maybe I could have pursued a respectable job or even gone to college. If prohibition didn't exist, possibly my job would be considered legitimate and there wouldn't be as much risk. If women already had the right to vote, to contraceptives, and to bodily autonomy, perhaps Claudia wouldn't be putting her life on the line. But this was our reality, and it tore me apart knowing that Claudia could be in danger and there was nothing I could do about it.

"Hey, they're getting ready to close," Thomas spoke up, breaking me out of my thoughts. "I'm going to try to coax the bartender to let us go upstairs for a beat."

"Thank you." It was all I could muster.

"Remind him about how we helped before the raid," James added.

Returning up the slanted ladder and seeing the table and chairs under the window, I couldn't help but think back to when Claudia and I sat there together.

We each grabbed a stack of papers and rifled through them. Well, Frank did after investigating the secret compartment, curiosity always getting the better of him.

"Their plans changed, right?" James asked for confirmation. "So instead of looking for their itinerary, what are we in search of?"

"See if we can find the contact information from overseas," Frank responded.

"I bet they'll have more information about what's possibly happened to the ship," Thomas added with hope.

The girls had a treasure trove of information up here. I think they may have also been acting as vigilantes for abuse survivors. I marked those items off as something to revisit with Claudia once we found her.

"Here!" James exclaimed, holding up a letter triumphantly. "It's from their contact overseas."

He handed it to me, and I realized with a sinking feeling that it was written in German.

"Does anyone happen to know German?" I asked, feeling defeated.

"The name and address is there," James said, his finger tapping the bottom of the crinkled page. "But it was these pictures that tipped me off." He gestured to the second page, where photographs of contraceptives were displayed.

"We could send a telegraph," Thomas suggested, his voice tinged with uncertainty.

"But how will they understand us if they only read German?" I voiced my concern.

"We could at least try," Frank interjected optimistically. "Maybe they know English."

"What if we can't trust them?" James posed a valid question. "What if they're the reason the boat has gone missing?"

"There is a German settlement not too far south of here," Frank offered. "Perhaps we could request their help and send a message under false pretenses."

"Oh, yes! Cole Camp!" Thomas exclaimed with a glimmer of hope in his eyes.

"But we would need to translate the message for the telegram once we reach there," James pointed out. "And we can't send an international telegram from that location."

"A journey to Cole Camp would cost both time and money too," Frank stated practically. "Why not first attempt a disguised message in English?"

We all pondered over the idea, my worry increasing with every passing moment.

"We'll try sending the telegram in English first," I finally decided, eager to take action. "If that doesn't work, then we'll head to Cole Camp." I was willing to do anything at this point.

"It's too late to go to the Western Union building now," James noted. "They must be closed."

"Maybe I can get us in," Thomas piped up, a hint of mischief in his tone. "I know someone on the cleaning staff." He shrugged nonchalantly.

"Does anyone here know how to send a telegram?" I asked, realizing none of us had ever done it before.

"I might be able to figure it out," Frank offered, always up for a challenge.

I couldn't help but feel grateful for my friends and their willingness to help. We donned our caps and got out of the bartender's way. Walking down the dimly lit streets at night was a familiar experience, but for some reason, on this particular night, it felt different. Perhaps it was because I was on edge, my gut telling me that something was amiss.

The sound of clanging metallic echoes came from an alleyway as we approached it. All of us stopped in our tracks. Then we heard yelling, and fear gripped my chest.

"I told him this was too dangerous."

"Yeah, but the payout is worth it." My heart raced as I recognized the second voice that spoke, Kris. His sly tone sent shivers down my spine. "We're due."

"Yeah, yeah, I know."

"Can't believe so many customers left to buy from Alex instead."

"Works out that Vernon's upset with him too."

"Sure does. He should be checking in soon."

"Can't believe the first ship wrecked!" His words caused dread to settle in my gut.

"Hope he got all of that bad luck out of his system."

Without hesitation, I marched forward, my friends following closely behind me. Thomas tried to stop me, but I shrugged off his hand determinedly. We needed answers, and we needed them right then.

"What ship?" I demanded, my voice shaking with anger, as I approached the men.

"Well, well, well," Kris taunted as he stepped out from the shadows. "Look who decided to show up." His smirk sent a wave of revulsion through me.

"It's the ship that's going to put you out of business," he gloated, his eyes glinting with malice.

I gritted my teeth, clenching my fists at my sides. "What's the ship's name?" I growled, ready to do whatever it took to get the information from him.

"What's it to you?" Kris snarled, his voice dripping with venom.

I lunged at him, ready to strike, when I saw the glint of a gun in his hand. My heart sank as I realized I was outmatched. Time seemed to stand still as we faced each other, both feeling combative.

James stepped in, disarming Kris and pulling me away before I could retaliate. Thomas and Frank held back Kris's friend, preventing him from joining the fight.

In a flash, I landed a punch to Kris's jaw, but he just smiled through the pain. He countered with a punch of his own, and we grappled on the ground, locked in a fierce struggle. Eventually, I managed to pin him down, but he laughed maniacally.

"What are you laughing at?" I demanded.

"Your sweet little lady is on that ship, isn't she?" he taunted.

"Just tell me the name of the ship!" I shouted, desperate for any piece of information.

"Fine," he relented with a smug smirk. "It's the Carroll A. Deering."

With a sigh of relief, I stood up, and James went to help Kris up. But instead, James shoved him away aggressively, fueled by anger and frustration. We quickly left the alley while Kris and his friend ran off in the opposite direction.

As they disappeared into the night, Kris shouted after us with one last jab: "Enjoy your evening!" And then he added another crucial detail: "Oh, and Vernon's next target is the S.S. Hewitt."

My heart raced as I realized we were running out of time to gather information about Claudia. It was now or never.

"We need to send that telegram immediately," I urged my team. "We have to act fast before Vernon strikes again."

As we approached the dark Western Union building, I noticed the second-floor lights were the only ones on, casting eerie shadows across the street. Thomas paced back and forth, peering through the windows until he spotted someone he recognized. He grabbed a few pebbles and threw them up one at a time, the sound of them ricocheting off the building floated down the street. The figure inside approached the window, waved, and then walked away.

The first floor lights flickered on and then Thomas's friend unlocked the door. She cracked it open. Her expression softened slightly at the sight of Thomas, but her gaze quickly traveled to me and my friends.

"What are you doing here?"

"Ceresa, I wanted to see you," Thomas replied.

"Who's with you?"

"Oh, these are my best buds."

She sighed.

"Can we come in for just a bit? We only need to warm up for a minute."

Her hesitation had me on edge, but I could only imagine what she was thinking.

"Fine, but be careful. If you break or take anything, I'll lose my job," she warned.

"We won't," Thomas reassured her. "I promise."

"Yeah, yeah." She huffed. "I need to get back to work."

As we entered the building, I couldn't help but notice how Thomas seemed to know his way around. He led Frank directly to the necessary office. Then Frank was drowning in the books on the shelves, searching for instructions.

"We have a limited number of words, so choose carefully," Frank spat out, his voice tense and urgent. "I'll figure out how to send the message. You prepare what you want to say."

Grabbing a fountain pen and paper, I sat at a desk. Instead of writing, I found myself staring at the curved wall, unable to come up with a single word. The building was splendid indeed, straight on one side and curved the rest of the way so that it formed a capital D if seen from above. But I didn't have time to focus on that, I had to find Claudia. It was crucial that my message conveyed all imperative information.

As Frank described how his father used railroad stations to telegraph in the past, he pinpointed the specific office we needed based on our found address. While he rambled on about automated teleprints and proper offices, the words finally came to me.

Watching my message being transmitted, I felt a surge of hope and relief ripple through me. Finally, some helpful news. But the wait for a response was agonizing. Every second felt like an eternity.

In that moment, my mind was consumed by misery and despair. The thought of losing Claudia was unbearable; it made it almost impossible to think clearly. Not again.

Losing my father had been devastating enough. I couldn't handle losing Claudia too. It would destroy me.

"It's here," James exclaimed, pulling me out of my spiraling thoughts. "We have a response."

I jumped up and hurried over to see what it said.

Frank's expression turned grave as he read it aloud.

Thomas removed his cap and held it to his chest, a solemn gesture.

James stepped in, trying to offer some hope. "Just because they don't know what happened to the ship doesn't mean it's completely lost."

Fueled by frustration and desperation, I stormed out of the building before anyone could stop me.

But then a thought struck me. Claudia knows Olinda. Why had I been seeking help from the wrong people this whole time? I should have begun my search by asking for women's help. I was going to see my mother. Time was running out, and I couldn't afford any more mistakes.

Armored Hours

Chapter Fifteen - Marie

Hansen 172

Let's take a step back, shall we? Just as quickly as Claudia had become close with me again, now she's disappeared. My friends, though, have been busy. While I've spoken with the men Claudia had been scheduled to meet, they've been keeping an eye on our possible counters. We've met at Olinda's tonight as she must remain near Alex's dear sick ma.

The atmosphere at Olinda's is tense and heavy, filled with worry and uncertainty. The flickering candles cast shadows on the walls, making the scene seem even more ominous. Olinda sits at the head of the table, her face etched with concern as she addresses the group.

"I have not noticed an aura around Alex," Olinda reports to the group, her voice strained with worry. "Only dismay as he watches his ma wither and absolute destruction as he falls apart in Claudia's absence."

While my sights had been fixed on Alex, it's hard to find error in Olinda's observations. She has always been perceptive and attuned to the world. I can't help but feel a wave of sadness for Alex and his family.

"I did witness an aura around Vernon," Anna chimes in, her tone serious and grave. "But he's been absent of late."

A shiver runs down my spine at her words. It seems too coincidental that Vernon would disappear at the same time as Claudia.

"I also witnessed an aura around Kris," Nelly adds gravely, her expression pained. "It was impossible to miss."

My breath catches in my throat at Nelly's revelation. She's the most skilled among us in seeing the mystical world, which only confirms my fears.

I am grateful for my friends' support and companionship during this trying time. They are fiercely loyal, and I know I can trust them with my life.

And now we have it—we know who the two counters are, Kris and Vernon. But the real challenge lies ahead; how can I ensnare the two beasts? How can I save my only remaining family in this world and lifetime? My thoughts race as I try to come up with a plan.

"Thank you, my dear friends," I say with deep gratitude. "Now we must draw a binding spell."

The kitchen erupts into action as we gather the necessary ingredients for the spell. We move about each other in a flurry, each of us focused on our task.

As we're collecting items for the spell, Alex rushes into the kitchen, looking frazzled and worried.

"Sorry to interrupt," the dear boy actually bows. "I need to draw a broth for Ma. I'll be out of your hair as quickly as I can."

He grabs a pot and begins his task but continues to speak to us no matter how busy his hands are. "So, any news on Claudia?" he asks, his voice filled with hope and desperation.

While he lacks the skill of subtlety, I don't miss his heartbroken eyes.

"That's exactly what we've been discussing," I cover.

"Has she written to you? Could there be possible clues that could help us?" he continues to press.

"I have them right here," I say, pulling out the letters from my purse.

Alex practically leaps out of his skin to retrieve the letters and pour over them eagerly. Meanwhile, my friends huddle together, whispering amongst themselves.

"Have you noticed the grace and chivalry with which Alex conducts himself?" Nelly's voice carries a hint of admiration as she speaks to me.

"My observations were brief, but I suppose so," I reply.

"He cares so deeply for his ma and see how tirelessly he searches for Claudia," Anna interjects, her tone filled with awe.

"And have you heard about his recurring experiences of déjà vu?" Olinda adds with wide eyes.

My gaze shifts back to Alex. Is it possible that he *is* reincarnated?

"We cannot say for certain," Anna confesses, her own past of being reincarnated unknown to her. "But he does exhibit many of the signs."

I start to speak, but am interrupted by Alex's polite voice. "Thank you all for letting me borrow the kitchen. Now, if you'll excuse me, I will take this broth to my ma."

As he exits, Olinda exclaims, "See, his manners are just as we said."

I mull over what she said in my mind but everything feels so uncertain. With Alex's departure, our focus returns to gathering the necessary ingredients for the binding spell. My friends begin humming a familiar tune, its lyrics bringing forth a distant memory from a future time. This song has since been remade into a ballad of finding love, causing realization to dawn on me—perhaps we have been focusing on the wrong spell all along. We may need a location spell as well.

"What is it?" Nelly asks, her hands full of candles.

"I need a moonlight stone, a feather, and some moss." Luckily, I happen to have one of Claudia's ribbons with me.

"A location spell," she deduces, her brows furrowed in concentration. "I like it."

Olinda chimes in with her practicality. "You'll need a map. We can't simply follow something over miles and an ocean on a whim."

Anna pipes up with curiosity. "How does it work with a map?"

I take a deep breath before explaining. "Once complete, this ribbon should hover and glow over Claudia's location."

As we begin to chant and conjure the binding spell, the energy in the air shifts and hums with power. It's a beautiful sight to see strong women come together for a common goal.

Inscribing the counters' names into each candle brings relief, but as we wrap thread around them, I sense a block in the spell. Something is interfering, and I can't quite pinpoint what it is.

"There's something blocking us," I inform my companions.

"Can that happen?" Anna asks, her voice filled with concern. "How?"

"It's possible," Olinda muses. "But no one knows that we're currently casting."

Nelly speaks up with determination. "I have an idea. Do you have any extra lavender rope rings?"

"Yeah?" Olinda responds hesitantly.

"We need to use each candle to burn a ring," Nelly exclaims excitedly. "That should break through the block."

And so, we do just that—burning the rings one by one as we resume our chanting. This time, the block is gone, and we're able to bind the counters from causing harm.

Now, all that's left is to locate Claudia and her friends. The anticipation and hope fills us as we continue using the power of magic.

We gather the stone, feather, and moss around the map. Once chanting again, I feel another block, but this one is much, much stronger. Its grip crushing and suffocating. As I strain against it, I feel myself being pulled away from my surroundings, dragged through a tunnel of darkness.

The room begins to spin and, when it finally stops, I find myself in a completely different place—my future home. I'm seated under a wooden pergola, surrounded by a lush garden bursting with colorful blooms. My vision is hazy, as though I am only spectating rather than fully present. Then, Claudia from this future timeline walks towards me, gracefully stepping on the stone pathway that leads to me.

The scent of blue hydrangeas, orange daffodils, and yellow roses fills the air as she sits next to me and wraps her arm around my shoulder. Despite her fuzzy appearance, it's comforting to have her here when she is missing in my current timeline. With a gentle squeeze of my shoulder, everything fades away, and my heart breaks as she dissolves into nothingness.

Next, I'm transported to a similar setting, but in a different timeline. Instead of colorful flowers, the air is filled with the scent of saltwater and fish. My eyes are drawn to a young woman who bears a striking resemblance to Claudia but who exists only in this dual future timeline. A sharp pain shoots through my stomach, causing me to double over.

This is new.

"I have a recipe book with precise instructions," the alternate Claudia states calmly.

I look out at the setting sun, which paints every wave with a shimmering layer of golden light. Some things never lose their beauty, whether they exist in the past or future, in a dual or organic timeline. Though I notice that sunsets do change slightly far into the distant future.

"Please take the bucket and book," the future Claudia says as she fades away into nothingness.

Abruptly, I am whisked away further into that distant future, where the sunsets are metallic, and nature is nowhere to be found.

I'm driving a poli-magno. The thrilling speed at which these futuristic cars drive is invigorating.

"Just don't," I say to the very futuristic Claudia. I'm upset with her in this timeline. Is that something that follows us through reincarnation? And why am I being thrown through them all right now?

Have the counters discovered that we've blocked them from harm? The thought makes my heart race. Are they playing games to get back at me? I need to return to my friends. I have to. I imagine Olinda's house and grip the poli-magno steering wheel as hard as I can, allowing adrenaline to snowball inside myself.

Olinda's place filters in, my vision becoming less and less blurry. It's muffled at first but I can hear my friends.

"Marie!" Anna says.

"Are you okay?" Olinda asks, concern etched on her face.

"Where'd you go?" Nelly doesn't miss much.

"My apologies," I say as I gather myself from the whirlwind. "We need to locate Claudia. The counters have figured out that we bound them."

"They're working against it?" Nelly asks incredulously.

I nod grimly.

"Then we must act quickly and get back to the location spell," Olinda, always quick on her feet, says.

The ribbon begins to hover over the map in front of us as soon as we're chanting. It lifts up two and then three inches. We all freeze but continue chanting. As soon as we know Claudia's location, we can save her. The benefit of being rich in this timeline is that I'm well connected and have the funds to hire a rescue party anywhere. All I need is her location.

With all my focus on the hovering ribbon, willing it to move towards Claudia's location, it suddenly freezes and shakes before falling back onto the map. My heart sinks like a deflated balloon. We must try again. We cannot lose her.

"What happened?" asks Anna, her voice trembling with worry. "Why'd it drop?"

Footsteps echo down the stairs. "I've poured over the letters but haven't found a single clue that can help." Alex looks up from the letters at us and sees the map we're circled around. "Oh, I'm interrupting again. I can come back."

Before he can fully turn away, the ribbon begins to elevate over the map once more. "Wait," I blurt out before I can think twice about it. "Maybe you can help us."

"Yes, please stay," Olinda invites Alex.

We don't usually allow outsiders into our magical circle like this, but desperate times call for desperate measures. We need all the help we can get. When we chant again, the ribbon moves further than before. It glides toward Texas, then over the gulf, and past Florida, where the ship last radioed in. It's working, but then it stops and shakes as if it will fall.

"Take my hand please," Anna requests of Alex.

Thankfully, he doesn't argue. We all clasp hands and continue our chant. The ribbon responds, moving closer and closer until it hovers over the Atlantic Ocean near Virginia. And then it finally glows.

My friends cheer and clap their hands.

"That's where she is?" Alex pleadingly asks. He's leaning over the map, memorizing the coordinates.

"We've found her!" Anna exclaims with tears in her eyes.

My friends gather around me for a hug. I hug them back and try to appear full of joy. But my joy is reserved. The ribbon didn't glow yellow like it should have. It glowed green and then blue.

That can only mean one thing. While it located Claudia's physical location, she's in an alternate universe, another world. Not just a different timeline. Somehow, my daughter's been taken to another realm altogether.

With determination etched onto his features, Alex breaks away from the group and snatches up his coat. It's clear that he has a singular purpose in mind as his eyes gleam with an unshakable resolve. While my friends debate over whom to contact first, I sense that Alex plans on taking matters into his own hands by physically going to the coordinates. He doesn't trust anyone else to save Claudia, and I can't blame him; the kid has a fierce loyalty and unwavering heart.

"Alex," I call out as I reach the door. "There's something important I need to tell you."

He halts in his tracks and regards me with a mixture of curiosity and doubt. How do I convey what he needs to know without revealing too much? Claudia mentioned having dreams of him in other timelines, something she had never experienced before. At first, I attributed it to the parallel timelines, but now I wonder if Alex has been the key all along. After all, our location spell only worked because of him.

"Yes?" he prompts. "What is it?"

"Claudia isn't exactly at the point on the map where we located her with the spell."

He rolls his eyes. "I thought I was supposed to be the skeptic when it comes to magic. But it worked and there's no way I'm not going to try to find her. You can't stop me."

"Do you really think I'd try to stop you?" I place a hand on his arm. "I want nothing more than for you to find her."

He looks confused, and I feel just as bewildered. When I touch him, I don't feel the usual tremor that comes with interacting with a reincarnated soul. It's usually so subtle that most people wouldn't even notice, but after years of being attuned to it, it's hard not to feel its absence.

"So, you're going to help me?" he asks, his expression a mix of astonishment and gratitude.

"Do you still have the lavender ring?" I query.

He nods, reaching for it in his pocket.

"Take it and here are a few more," I instruct and hand him more rings. "When you get to the location, light the rings on fire."

"Um, okay?" He contemplates my suggestion for a moment before nodding again. "I'll do anything to find her." With that declaration, he storms off, exuding a fierce determination that brings to mind only one other person—my sister's beloved through many lifetimes. Perhaps this is a good sign. Perhaps Alex is the only one who can stand against him.

CHAPTER SIXTEEN – CLAUDIA

RUSH AFTER IT FULL OF ANGER
CAUSE YOUR ADRENALINE LEVEL TO SPIKE
TAKE A FEW DEEP BREATHS
THEN CHARGE
THAT'S HOW ONE TRAVELS

The knife Kiersten had thrown with swiftness and precision landed directly through Vernon's trigger finger, removing it and simultaneously locking the gun. The sound of his bellowing filled the air, even over the ship's alarms still blaring, as he crumpled to the ground in pain. The girls watched in shock and bewilderment at what had just transpired.

"Bloody hell," a crew member said as he ran up to Vernon. "Better get you to the medic."

More crew members frantically ran by them. Kiersten nonchalantly shrugged her shoulders, following after the commotion. Kiersten's quick movements snapped the rest of the girls out of their frozen state, and they all ran after her.

When they reached the deck of the ship, they couldn't believe their eyes. They had been miles out at sea not too long ago, but now they were miraculously near a coastline. A stone stairway stood in the middle of the beach, beckoning to them with an almost magical pull. It seemed as though even the birds flying above could feel the emotional weight of this place.

Claudia shielded her eyes from the bright sun and pointed excitedly to a man standing on the shore.

"Look there," she said to her friends. "He doesn't look like my father, but he feels like my father."

The man waved to the ship, his features becoming clearer as they approached.

"Well, whoever he is, it seems like he knows you too," Lina commented with a raised eyebrow. "Or he's just being polite. Are you sure you didn't hit your head, Claudia?"

"Where are we?" Kiersten asked, still trying to process everything that was happening.

"What is this place?" Florian echoed, glancing around with a sense of unease. "It feels…strange, doesn't it?"

Claudia nodded in agreement. "It does feel like a different world."

The man on the coast caught their attention as he carefully placed a rolled-up piece of paper into a bottle and corked it. Then, the man did something odd. With a surprisingly strong huff of breath, he sent the bottle out to sea towards their ship. It was almost unsettling how easily he could manipulate the waves and currents with just his breath. There was something almost magical about it.

Claudia's heart raced as she squinted against the bright sunlight reflecting off the water. With determination in her eyes, she dashed towards a small net hoist on the deck, her friends trailing behind in bewilderment as their feet pounded against the wooden deck floor.

The bottle glinted in the sunlight, its contents beckoning to Claudia. She reached out and carefully retrieved it, her fingers trembling with anticipation. With eager hands, she unfurled the paper inside.

"What does it say?" Lina eagerly asked.

Florian's voice trembled as she took a seat on a nearby crate, feeling lightheaded from the sudden turn of events. "I'll fetch you some water," Kiersten called out before rushing away.

Despite the strange world they had found themselves in and the unsettling effects it seemed to have on Florian, hope filled Claudia as she read the words on the paper. "It says we have to meditate in order to return to our world," she announced to her friends. "My mother taught me how."

"Okay," Lina said, sounding uncertain. "What do we do? How do we meditate?"

"We need to sit and relax, take deep breaths," Claudia explained.

"That sounds refreshing," Kiersten remarked as she returned with water for Florian.

But Florian hesitated, worried about ruining her attire by sitting on the dirty wood. "Do you want to stay in this world?" Claudia pressed.

"Yeah," Kiersten chimed in. "Look at the pants that man on the beach is wearing. I doubt their fashion matches yours."

With a sigh, Florian finally joined them and crossed her legs reluctantly.

"Close your eyes and inhale deeply," Claudia instructed.

As they followed her lead they were abruptly jolted back into reality by a loud splash. Their eyes shot open, and Claudia quickly turned her head in the opposite direction of her friends, hoping they hadn't noticed her momentary lapse. Half a dozen sailors had apparently jumped ship and were now swimming towards shore without even bothering to grab a small boat.

"What are they doing?" Claudia asked a nearby crew member, realizing that their chances of returning to their world on the ship and finishing their goal were dwindling. She couldn't help but hope that Vernon, the troublesome cop who had lost a finger due to his reckless behavior, was among those abandoning ship. But she also knew that he could come back seeking revenge at any moment.

The crew member's words hung heavy in the air, punctuated by the soft lapping of waves against the side of the ship. "They want to stay," he said, his voice strained with desperation. "Tired of the harsh working conditions onboard and believe this to be paradise."

Claudia furrowed her brow, taking in the scene before her. The sun was setting over the horizon, casting a warm orange glow over everything. But she knew this was no paradise.

"You try stopping them," the man continued, gesturing towards the group of men eagerly making their way to the stairs. "It's impossible."

Kiersten tapped Claudia on the shoulder, pulling her out of her thoughts. "Look, the man's trying to stop them from ascending the stairs."

Sure enough, the man who had reminded Claudia of her father was desperately trying to block their path.

"Stop!" Claudia yelled out, but it was too late. They had already punched him, and he was now sprawled on the ground. With excited grins on their faces, the men raced up the stairs like schoolboys at the end of the last day before summer break.

As they ascended, one by one they began to disappear as if they were clouds dissipating into thin air.

"What's happening to them?" Lina asked, her eyes wide with fear.

"They're crossing over to heaven," the crew member said solemnly before quickly running across the deck and jumping into the ocean.

Claudia and her friends sat back down, still reeling from what they'd just witnessed. They crossed their legs and took deep breaths, trying to process it all. Slowly, darkness began to envelop them as if thunderous clouds had rolled in.

Then, as Claudia's eyes closed, a faint violet circle appeared in her vision. She couldn't tell if it was on her eyelids or in her mind's eye.

"Do you all see that?" Florian asked, awe and wonder evident in her voice. "I've never seen a purple like this before."

"Me either," Kiersten chimed in, her own amazement mirroring Florian's.

"Claudia, is this normal?" Lina's voice trembled with fear and uncertainty.

Claudia took a deep breath and tried to steady herself. "Yes, please keep your eyes closed, straighten your backs, and breathe," she instructed her friends. "In and out. Concentrate."

Gradually, the noise from the men around them faded away until all they could hear was the soft lapping of waves. And then, once again, the violet circle appeared, followed by another brilliant blue one within it. Claudia felt weightless as she let herself be carried away by the sensation. It was like her body moving forward and then her brain catching up, similar to how walking felt right after she went severely deaf in one ear.

"Now, open your eyes," commanded Claudia to her friends. They slowly blinked, their eyes adjusting from prolonged closure.

"It's dark," remarked Kiersten as she observed their new surroundings.

"We must still be in the same place," Lina said with disappointment.

"Something went wrong," exclaimed Florian. "We're still by a coastline. Look at the bonfire over there."

They all followed her gaze and saw a blazing fire on the shore. The remaining sailors around them marched off the ship in a trance-like state, before diving into the water and swimming towards the bonfire.

"I can see a lighthouse too," added Kiersten, squinting her eyes until they fully adjusted to the darkness.

As the sailors reached the shore, they were handed candles, which they lit up one by one. Suddenly, there was a gunshot, and the lighthouse began flashing a distress signal. Claudia and her friends held onto each other tightly, their hearts racing with fear.

"What's happening?" asked Lina, her voice trembling.

In the dim light, they could make out more figures near the lighthouse, some wearing shining armor that glinted in the moonlight. Claudia felt a strong presence emanating from them.

"We need to get out of here," stated Claudia with concern. "Something doesn't feel right."

"You don't have to tell me twice," agreed Kiersten. "I'll go retrieve the items we came for in the first place."

"And we'll gather our luggage," added Lina, pointing at herself and Florian. "So we're ready to disembark from this ship of horrors as soon as we return to our world."

"Are you speaking for me now?" Florian said. "Are you sure we're in another world?"

"But look at that boat approaching the lighthouse," pointed out Claudia. "That's not from our world. Plus, you're no longer lightheaded, are you?"

"Well, it doesn't feel that different from our world"—Florian paused—"but you're right about the boat."

As the others left Claudia on the deck, she couldn't help but notice a figure standing on the lighthouse catwalk. For some reason, they felt familiar to her, almost like Anna. But as she looked closer, a shadowy figure appeared beside the familiar one, and a sense of foreboding washed over her.

Piercing shrieks and haunting howls echoed through the stillness, sending chills down Claudia's spine. She instinctively covered one ear, trying to muffle the unsettling noises, though they didn't really compete with her tinnitus.

The other hand remained free, ready to take on any task that may require it. Perhaps there was more to the letter from the bottle. With a trembling hand, she unfurled the damp paper and read it once again. A postscript caught her eye, mentioning a ritual that could help them now.

Just as Claudia's friends returned from retrieving their items, she felt a sense of relief wash over her. Their familiar faces and voices lifted some of the gloom that had settled upon her.

"Do you all have the lavender rings I gave you?" Claudia asked, trying to sound nonchalant.

"I have mine," Kiersten replied. "And I've been wearing it like you suggested."

"Same here," Florian added with a small smile. "Even though it clashes with my outfit."

Lina lifted her hand to show off her own ring. "I never take mine off."

"There was more to the letter," Claudia revealed with a hint of urgency in her voice. "We have to burn these rings."

"But why?" Lina asked, with confusion etched on her face. "I thought they protected us."

"It's part of a ritual that should take us back," Claudia answered confidently.

"We can do this," Kiersten encouraged, determination shining in her eyes.

"Thankfully, I happen to have matches with me," Florian chimed in, producing a small matchbox from her pocket.

As they gathered around, they witnessed sparks dance in the air from the bonfire and flames leap higher, as if fueled by an invisible force. It was a frenzy near the lighthouse, and Claudia felt the gloom return.

The wind picked up, blowing fiercely across the ship and causing it to lurch from side to side. Water sprayed over the ship, raining horizontally against them. Claudia and her friends held onto each other tightly as they scrambled to collect their belongings.

"Do you still have your rings?" Claudia asked her friends anxiously.

They all felt around their fingers and confirmed that they still had their lavender rings.

"They're soaked," Lina remarked, holding up her dripping hand.

"As are my matches," Florian added, disappointment evident in her voice.

"This is just great," Kiersten grumbled. "What do we do now?"

Claudia noticed lights flickering in the distance, further out in the water than they were.

"Wait," Florian said, rummaging through her purse. "I think I may have a lighter."

"Look!" Claudia pointed excitedly at the lights that had caught her eye.

"Is it another ship?" Lina asked hopefully. "Maybe they could help us."

"But it's hazy," Kiersten pointed out. "Even the lights look like they're behind a thick fog."

One of the lights lifted and waved back and forth.

"Are they signaling to us?" Claudia asked. The gloom feeling was gone and replaced by another, home! *Could it be?* Claudia could scarcely believe it. "I think it's Alex."

"How is that possible?" Lina asked incredulously. "Is he here in this other world too? How did he get here?"

"No, that must be why he's fuzzy," Kiersten reasoned. "He's physically at this location, but in our world, not this one."

"I knew he would come looking for us," Claudia said with a wistful smile.

"I found it," Florian exclaimed, finally lifting the lighter out of her purse.

"Oh, thank goodness," Lina breathed a sigh of relief. "We can finally escape this eerily strange place."

"Wait, his light is flashing," Claudia said as she took hold of Florian's arm that held the lighter.

"Lover boy is sending a message"—Florian exclaimed—"how sweet."

"Let me see if I can decipher it," Lina said. "It looks like morse code."

Lina spoke aloud, counting the flashing dots and dashes, Kiersten helping her keep track. Lina seemed to be back in her natural habitat, calculations, and her friends were glad of it.

"So?" Kiersten prompted eagerly once Lina had finished.

"It's something about lighting together," Lina said, deep in thought. "But what could it mean?"

Just then, Claudia saw a small flame alight from the boat. "Quick, ignite the lighter, Florian."

Florian struck the lighter to life, and a bright flame erupted. "As you wish."

"Alex is going to burn his rings at the same time we burn ours," Claudia realized with excitement.

One by one, they put their rings in the flame. It took a minute for each to burn as they were still soaked. Claudia's heart beat frantically in her chest as she anxiously watched Alex, hoping his pace would match theirs. But his flame flickered out too quickly for her liking, sending a surge of fear through her body. Did he finish before them?

As they remained trapped in this other world, Alex's boat still obscured by a hazy mist, another flame came to life on the deck. Relief flooded through Claudia as she realized he must be using matches instead of a lighter—perhaps their pacing would align naturally.

As the last ring sizzled and disintegrated in the flames, the sun all of a sudden burst forth, blinding them and igniting a sense of hope deep within the girls. They clung to each other, jumping up and down in jubilation at the sight of Alex rowing toward them with newfound clarity. Claudia could barely contain her excitement as she joined the others in gathering themselves for his arrival.

"Wait, we can't make it anywhere on his little boat," Kiersten said, reality crashing down on her.

"He must have come on a ship," Lina observed. "Didn't make it all the way here on that tiny vessel."

"They abandoned him," Florian pointed out. "He risked everything to be with you." She looked at Claudia.

Tears pricked at Claudia's eyes as she struggled to hold back her emotions. She took a deep breath and tried to compose herself. "Perhaps he can figure out how to steer this rig."

"We can help," Kiersten added, putting an arm around Claudia. "And maybe a couple of the crew members remain."

They dropped a ladder down to Alex, and he climbed as quickly as his body would allow. Claudia and him embraced as soon as he was onboard. Alex breathed in Claudia's scent, happy she was alive and well. She kissed his cheek once, twice, and a third time.

Bootsteps echoed behind them. "Oh look, it's everyone I want to arrest all gathered nice and neat together for me." It was Vernon. "Arrest them!"

Armored Hours

CHAPTER SEVENTEEN – ALEX

S.S. HEWITT UNDER THE COMMAND OF
CAPTAIN HANS JAKOB HANSEN
RADIOED IN JANUARY 25TH AS SCHEDULED
BUT HAS NOT BEEN HEARD FROM AGAIN
A HUGE SEARCH ALONG HER ROUTE FOUND
NOTHING

Of all the bad luck, it seemed as though fate had conspired to bring Vernon on board the same ship as Claudia and her friends. Despite my efforts to find them and hold Claudia in my arms for just a brief moment, our reunion was cut short by none other than Vernon—my least favorite and the most corrupt cop.

As his men handcuffed us, Vernon turned to Kiersten with a wicked grin. "Be sure to rid this one of her knives," he ordered.

I couldn't help but notice that Vernon's right hand was bandaged. I made a mental note to ask Kiersten about it later.

"And we'll need to take the birth control with their things too," he added with a smirk. "It's evidence against these ladies."

Florian immediately protested, but Vernon silenced her with a sharp glare. "Be quiet," he barked before turning back to his men while pointing at me. "And as for the booze we've been after, this one will be charged for bootlegging it, and we'll confiscate it as evidence."

Lina winced as one of the men grabbed her arm a little too hard. I let out a grunt when another shoved me forward.

We were all escorted down to a lower level, passing by cramped crew cabins until we reached what appeared to be an office of sorts. A couple desks lined the far walls, their surfaces cluttered with papers and other various items. Underneath a porthole window sat a long pipe, which we were promptly handcuffed to.

Once Vernon and his men left, I let out a sigh of relief at the absence of his grating voice. But looking around at the worried expressions on Claudia and her friends' faces, I knew we were in trouble. As luck would have it, I was positioned at one end of the group and used my foot to scoot a chair toward Lina, who was next to me. Of course, Vernon had strategically placed Claudia at the opposite end, knowing how we felt about each other.

As soon as she saw me, Claudia flashed a small smile and used her foot to push a chair toward Florian. Kiersten, stuck in the middle, opted to perch on the pipe and lean against the wall for support.

"No, wait," Claudia urgently exclaimed. "That pipe might not hold you."

Kiersten just grinned mischievously and waggled her eyebrows. "Would that be so bad?"

The absurdity of the situation actually made me chuckle. Despite everything, Claudia and her friends couldn't help but laugh along with me.

"How are we going to get out of this?" Florian asked with a hint of desperation. "Jail really isn't my style."

Lina furrowed her brow in concentration before suggesting, "Maybe there's a letter opener in one of the desks."

With a determined look on her face, Claudia stretched out her leg and managed to pull open the middle desk drawer with her foot. "I see one, but I'm not sure if I can reach it."

"Try yanking the whole drawer out," I encouraged. I reached my foot out too, but the desk nearest to me appeared to be locked.

But Claudia's efforts paid off as the drawer flew across the floor and landed with a thud in front of Kiersten. She gracefully hopped down from her seat on the pipe, extended her leg to pull the drawer closer, and retrieved the letter opener. She moved like a contortionist, dragging the letter opener with her foot. Then she picked it up with both feet while she hung from the pipe with one arm to retrieve it with her other hand. With nimble fingers, she deftly inserted the sharp blade into her handcuffs and began to wiggle it around. The rest of us held our breaths in anticipation.

Finally, there was a satisfying *click*, and Kiersten's handcuffs released her from their grasp. But before we could celebrate, I spoke up.

"Wait," I said urgently.

"What? No way," Kiersten protested as she moved on to Florian's restraints.

"We're still too far away from shore," I explained. "Vernon will surely check on us before we reach land, and they'll just lock us up again and retrieve the letter opener."

Kiersten paused, considering my words. "You forget about my knife skills." She grinned slyly as she lifted the letter opener once more.

"But they have guns," I reminded her.

"True," Kiersten conceded with a nod. "Although if it were just one gun, it would be no problem."

I raised an eyebrow in surprise.

"Did you notice Vernon's bandaged hand?" Claudia interjected.

"That was you? Why did I have a feeling?" I exclaimed, pointing accusingly at Kiersten.

"I took a finger and disarmed him at the same time," she replied nonchalantly, even giving a small curtsy.

"Note to self: do not anger Kiersten," I quipped humorously.

"But realistically," Lina cut in with a sensible suggestion. "We should put the drawer back and lock ourselves up again, but keep the letter opener hidden."

"Uh, really?" Florian's discomfort with remaining restrained was clear.

"Or, we could simply find a good hiding spot," Claudia offered as an alternative.

"Yes, that would be a much better plan," Florian agreed.

"One problem," I interjected. "How would we deboard without being caught?"

"Fine!" Kiersten exclaimed with frustration, cleaned up the drawer, slammed it back in place, and returned to the pipe. Once she was handcuffed again, the letter opener disappeared.

"Where'd it go?" I asked her.

"A lady never reveals her hiding spots."

"Since we're stuck here for a while, I'd love to hear more about your knife skills, Kiersten. I'd also like to know how you all disappeared. Your ship blipped off the map."

"Honestly, it was a mystery," Lina said with a shrug. "I'm not sure we can explain it."

"Maybe just tell me about your experience," I suggested. "Start from the beginning."

"Okay, as you know, our trip was delayed," Claudia started. "Getting to the ship proved harder than we thought it would be. I almost drowned from a forceful wave."

Every ounce of my being wanted to go to her and comfort her. Even my heart clenched at the thought of Claudia struggling against powerful waves. Maybe I had Kiersten keep us locked up earlier than I should have.

"But we made it aboard eventually," Florian continued. "Kiersten became acquainted with the kitchen staff while we settled in, but she came back with news."

"As Kiersten joined us in our room, she told us she thought she saw Vernon," Lina continued.

"We got the crew on our side to help us collect the birth control in secret," Kiersten said. "And then we went to spy on Vernon."

I was impressed with their actions. They were smart and brave. Unfortunately, Vernon was evil and manipulative.

"But he caught us," Claudia said, her voice trembling in fear at the memory. "He pulled his gun on us."

"To which I threw my knife, severing his trigger finger and locking his gun from use at the same time." Kiersten was proud of herself, and I couldn't find a reason to argue for her not to be. I was proud of her too.

"But how did you disappear?" I prodded.

"As Kiersten expertly displayed her skills, my attention was solely focused on the glint of Vernon's gun in his hand," Claudia recounted. "The rush of adrenaline from my concern for my friends was both terrifying and exhilarating, propelling me forward as I charged towards him."

"The next thing we knew, the ship suddenly tilted and threw us off balance, causing the lights to flicker, as if something or someone were interfering with their power," Lina explained.

"We followed the frantic crew up to the deck to see what was happening," Florian added. "And what we saw was beyond belief. We were now by the shore when mere seconds ago, we had been miles away at sea."

"And everything felt so different," Claudia interjected. "It was as if we could sense the emotions of every being around us—animals, humans, even objects."

"So it was another world?" I asked incredulously. "That's why I had to burn the rings to fully see you without the fog obscuring my vision?"

"There's more to it than that," Kiersten replied cryptically.

Just then, the door flew open, interrupting her. "Just checking on my little inmates," Vernon said cheerfully. "Ah yes, seeing you all locked up gives me such joy."

None of us spoke a word.

"Fine. Have it your way." Vernon huffed before slamming the door shut behind him.

"Please continue," I urged Kiersten.

"We tried meditating in an attempt to return to our own world," Kiersten continued. "But instead of bringing us back here, it transported us to yet another unfamiliar place."

"This new world didn't have the strange sensations like the previous one did, but it did have things that clearly didn't belong in our time period," Lina added.

"Wait a minute, now I remember something," Claudia exclaimed. "That first world we were in, it's also in the future. I remember that beach now from a dream. I could even feel the emotions of the sand particles as I stood on the shore."

"Actually," I interjected as I remembered a perplexing thought, "I also had a dream where you told me about feeling the emotions of sand particles before."

"You have?" Claudia looked at me longingly.

"What about the second place?" Lina inquired, while looking at Claudia.

"Well, it felt familiar, but I don't remember dreaming about it."

"Tell me more about it," I urged, eager to learn more.

"There was a gaudy bonfire next to a lighthouse," Florian shared.

"I do remember a lighthouse in a dream," my response came quickly, the memory flooding back. "There was someone on the catwalk and loud, ghostly howls."

"That's it exactly." Claudia gasped, her face lit up in realization.

As the ship slowed down, we all swayed away from the pipe. It must have meant that we were nearing our stop.

"I think we're getting close to the end of the journey," Lina announced confidently.

"How are we going to escape this ship without getting thrown in jail?" Kiersten's desperation was palpable.

"Claudia's mom plans to be there when we anchor, and I'm willing to bet she'll have plenty of resources with her," I reassured them.

"She is?" Claudia asked in surprise.

"Oh, splendid," Florian chimed in. "I do hope she brings a change of clothes as well."

"So she'll bail us out and hire lawyers for our cases?" Lina asked.

"I believe so," I confirmed. "She's the one who told me to burn the lavender rings to find you."

We could hear the activity of the remaining crew as they moved about the ship.

Kiersten unlocked herself from her restraints once again.

"What are you doing?" Lina asked, eyeing her warily.

"You lot might trust the rich, but I don't," Kiersten answered bluntly. "Sure, Claudia's mother will look out for her, but I doubt she'll go out on a limb for the rest of us."

While I'd recently witnessed kindness from Marie, previously, I'd felt the very same as Kiersten. "I believe she's changed. Perhaps her previous indifference had been a ruse."

"Well, I'm not taking any chances." Kiersten turned to Lina, handed her the letter opener, and instructed how to remove the cuffs. Then she turned to Florian and did the same as she produced a second opener I didn't realize she had acquired. She surprised me by handing a third and a fourth to Claudia and myself. Finally, she locked herself back up.

Vernon burst into the room, his heavy footsteps thudding against the hardwood floor. He sauntered up to Claudia, a sinister smirk playing across his lips.

"You know," he drawled, pushing Claudia's hair behind her ear, "I could let you go."

"Leave her alone," I shouted, my voice cracking with fear and anger.

But Vernon paid me no mind as he stepped toward me. In one swift motion, his fist collided with my jaw, sending searing pain through my head.

"As for you," he sneered, "you'll be paying for your crimes for a long time. Maybe even forever."

"No!" Claudia screamed in a sudden fit of rage.

"Take them away," Vernon bellowed to the other officers who had entered the room. Following closely behind them was someone I despised just as much as Vernon—Kris.

"What are you doing here?" I seethed, knowing that he must have been involved in all of this somehow. They were working together.

Kris raised his gun and pointed it directly at me. My heart raced as I heard a few clicks and then the sound of metal clanging against metal.

"Not so fast," Claudia snarled at Kris.

"Restrain them!" Vernon commanded his team.

The first officer to step forward received a heavy fountain pen deeply embedded in his thigh, thanks to Kiersten's quick reflexes and expert precision.

The second officer fared no better as Florian delivered a knockout punch with ease. I couldn't believe she would risk breaking a nail, even in the midst of this chaos.

But Lina surprised me the most. As the third officer lunged towards her, she gracefully dodged his attack, grabbing hold of his body and using her momentum to somersault backwards. With a resounding thud, she slammed his head against the hard floor.

"That's enough!" Vernon roared, trying to regain control.

"I've got this," Kris said confidently. He had lowered his gun in the midst of the commotion, but now he lifted it again—directly at me.

My heart stopped as I realized that this might be it. And it would all be at the hands of the asshole named Kris Mardell.

But just as he pulled the trigger, Claudia's voice snapped me out of my shock.

"No!" she screamed, diving in front of me to take the bullet meant for me. My heart shattered as she fell to the ground.

In a fit of rage and grief, I lunged at Kris and managed to wrestle his gun away from him before knocking him unconscious with it.

The other girls sprang into action, using their handcuffs to detain each officer in turn—Lina with her signature somersault maneuver, Florian with her precise punch, and Kiersten with her swift movements and expert aim.

Vernon reached for a gun with his uninjured hand, but it wasn't his dominant one, and he was slow.

"Drop it before you lose another finger," Kiersten said, while holding a letter opener.

With a resigned expression, he did as instructed, and she secured him with his comrades on the pipe.

We all turned to Claudia. Lina dropped to her knees beside her to assess the wound. Kiersten and Florian were by her side in a heartbeat, their faces fraught with concern.

I stood there, frozen in fear and disbelief, as I watched the woman I loved bleed out on the floor. Once again, Claudia had acted selflessly—this time taking an actual bullet meant for me. My heart raced with guilt and regret. It was all my fault that she lay there fighting for her life. The weight of my actions bore down on me like a heavy stone, threatening to crush me under its weight.

Armored Hours

Chapter Eighteen - Marie

Hansen 214

A sharp vise tightens around my heart, constricting and causing waves of pain to radiate throughout my entire body. My back, arms, neck, and jaw ache with a severe intensity. The weight in my chest is heavy and unrelenting, squeezing me from the inside out. It feels like something truly horrific is happening. If it weren't for the mystical tinge that accompanies these sensations, I might believe I was having a heart attack. But because magic is intertwined with every feeling I'm experiencing, I can't help but fear that someone I care about has been tragically injured.

My friends sitting next to me on the train show no signs of discomfort. Nelly reads Anna's palm while Anna gazes out at the scenery rushing by outside the windows. Olinda is lost in her book, completely at ease. However, when she senses me looking at her, she lifts her head.

"What's wrong?" she asks.

"It's Claudia," I manage to say between gasps for air. "She's hurt."

"We'll get to her as quickly as we can. Take some deep breaths," Olinda suggests calmly.

But let's backtrack for a moment and take a closer look at how we got here. There may be a solution hidden within the details.

We knew, based on a location spell, that we needed to take a train ride east. But we had no idea which port our destination lay in, or if Claudia and her friends would even make it there at all.

Our first stop was Chicago, where we met up with our friend Rose, a skilled crystal witch who we hoped could help us find the place we were seeking. She had been part of the group that helped ratify the Nineteenth Amendment and was known for her inventive solutions to impossible situations.

"Hello there, fellow wicked women," Rose greeted us, her tone dripping with friendly sarcasm.

"My dear, how have you been?" I responded with exaggerated politeness, playing along with our inside joke.

We embraced in a hug, and she beckoned for Olinda, Nelly, and Anna to join us. It was quite a sight—five intelligent and independent women coming together in joy.

"You all look famished," Rose said, dropping the sarcasm. "Come to my place, have a drink, and rest after your journey."

At the word "drink," Olinda glanced around nervously to make sure no one was eavesdropping. I couldn't help but wonder what she would do if someone had overheard.

As we settled into Rose's home, Nelly's gaze lingered on the crystals adorning her shelves. Her innate psychic abilities were drawn to their energy, amplifying and attracting it like a magnet. Witches like Rose possessed the power to manifest and manipulate energy with ease.

"Thank you for welcoming us into your home," Anna said warmly, her thoughtful consideration always touching me deeply.

"It is my pleasure. Although I must ask my dear friend, Marie, a few questions," Rose replied with a slight furrow of her brow.

"Go ahead," I urged.

"What's with all the counters lately? I glimpsed the aura of one weeks ago and another just a couple days before your arrival."

"So, you did see them," I confirmed, knowing they would probably come through Chicago. "Did you happen to get a sense of where they were headed?"

"No, but I could sense that while at first they were under a binding spell, presumably by you and your friends, they have since broken free from it," Rose divulged.

"That's not good at all," Olinda interjected. "And how do you know about counters—all of this?"

A knowing look passed between me and Rose. "Marie and I have been friends for many lifetimes," she revealed calmly.

"How have I never seen this in all of the fortunes I've read?" Nelly exclaimed in amazement.

"It is well-protected," I explained quickly, wanting to steer the conversation back on track. With the counters now roaming freely and potentially causing harm, my priority was finding Claudia before it was too late. "We can discuss all of this in detail later. Right now, let's focus on finding out where the counters are headed."

Rose retrieved a basket filled with candles and distributed them to each of us. "Please sit in a circle on the rug over there," she instructed.

We gathered around and took our candles, while Rose produced a box of matches from her pocket.

"We don't need those," Olinda declared, lifting her hands and causing the candles to ignite simultaneously. She began to chant:

"Fire of old, burn

Seasons of time, turn

Power of light, glow

Passion of love, flow."

The flames flickered and danced in response to her words.

"Now that's wickedly beautiful," Rose responded. "Do you have anything of theirs?"

"Um, no, is that okay?" Anna asked, worried.

"You at least know their names, right?" Rose pushed.

"Yes"—Nelly jumped in—"they're Vernon and Kris."

Rose's voice resonated through the room, commanding our attention as she began the ritual. "Raise your candles," she instructed, her words carrying a hint of reverence. "Repeat after me: this circle is blessed by fire." We followed her lead, feeling the warmth and power of the flames in our hands.

"Now say their names with me six times: Vernon, Kris; Vernon, Kris…" The air around us seemed to shift and change, as if responding to our incantation. A gentle breeze swept through the open windows, bringing with it the distant sound of waves crashing against a shore. And then, like a haunting melody drifting in on the wind, the faint ringing of a bell reached our ears.

A sense of anticipation filled the room as we waited for a sign to guide us towards our destination. Remarkably, a small but determined chickadee flew into our circle and perched itself at its center. "The symbol of guidance and bravery," I whispered, feeling a surge of hope within me.

But as we continued to concentrate, another visitor appeared. This time, it was a tabby cat that seemingly materialized out of thin air and locked its gaze upon us. Rose stood up and approached the door, and without hesitation or explanation, the bird and cat followed her out into the hallway.

Puzzled but undeterred, Olinda spoke up. "Wait…do you remember those women we met at last year's national convention here in Chicago?" Nelly and I glanced at each other before nodding in response. "Two of them were discussing secret symbols used by the suffragettes in their respective states."

Understanding dawned on Nelly's face as she connected the dots. "You're right…the chickadee and tabby cat are symbols for Massachusetts," she declared with certainty. Our mission had suddenly become clearer, aided by this serendipitous encounter with these powerful symbols in a place of magic and mystery.

"That's where we need to go," I said with confidence. "Boston."

"Well, looks like you'll have to catch another train," Rose commented. "I'll pack you some food for the journey."

Rose quickly whipped up delicious tea sandwiches and packed them in a small picnic basket. She truly was a blessing; her magical abilities helped us gather the information we desperately needed.

Before we knew it, we had purchased our tickets and boarded the train headed for Boston. I could only hope that it would move faster.

I was sitting next to Anna, while Nelly and Olinda had fallen asleep in their seats.

"Could you please pass me one of those sandwiches?" Anna asked politely.

I handed her one and grabbed one for myself as well.

"Rose is quite the chef," she remarked between bites.

"She really is," I agreed.

We ate our sandwiches in content silence.

"Did I ever tell you that my late husband was a railroad man?" Anna asked me.

"No, I don't believe so," I replied, intrigued by this new piece of information about her past.

"I lost him in a carriage accident, but lately he's been appearing in my dreams."

"In a positive way?" I quirked my eyebrow, hoping to add some humor to the conversation and make Anna more comfortable sharing.

"Oh no." She chuckled. "Just happy memories from our time together."

"Do you often have vivid dreams like this?" I asked curiously.

"No, not usually. But these ones feel so real. Some have even occurred in life after…not the ones with my late husband, of course."

I reached out and took her hand, sensing there was more to her story.

"Remember when you told us about how you're reincarnated?" Anna continued. "Lately, I've been experiencing déjà vu a lot. Isn't that a sign of reincarnation?"

I nodded, tears springing to my eyes and my throat tightening. "I know you're reincarnated because I'm the one who made it possible."

Anna pulled her hand away, but I grasped it back firmly.

"What did you do? And why?" she asked, confusion evident in her voice.

"I couldn't bear to lose you because you're my sister, and I love you," I confessed with a heavy heart.

"I'm what? How?"

The shock was palpable in her voice as she struggled to process the information.

"We first lived hundreds of years ago. You fell in love with a powerful man and when you joined him on a dangerous mission, you lost your life."

Her chest heaved with rapid breaths as realization dawned on her.

"In fact, I think he's the one who sent the counters. At first, I thought they were targeting you, but all the timelines changed. Claudia did something to subvert his plans far in the future."

Anna's expression twisted in confusion and betrayal. "Why would the man I love do such horrific things?"

"That is a long and complicated story, but the gist of it is that losing you shattered him. He spiraled into madness over and over again throughout time."

We were both silent after that as she thought over what I said.

"I think I need a drink," Anna said, breaking the tense silence.

Nelly chimed in, "That sounds like an excellent idea." She and Olinda stirred from their slumber.

"Did you sleep well?" I asked, trying to change the subject.

"Yes, I even had dreams," Olinda responded with a wistful smile.

Anna and I exchanged knowing glances.

"Did you know that the most common word people utter before they die is 'mother', 'ma', or some variation thereof?" Olinda asked.

"Is that what you dreamed about?" I asked with concern.

"Of course they do," Nelly interjected. "Feminine energy is full of love, which is why it's naturally the most powerful. And it's also why masculine energy constantly tries to control it."

"Wives have to list themselves as 'wife of' instead of using their own names on passports," Anna added bitterly.

"Law firms still refuse to hire women who've graduated from law school," I added angrily.

Olinda huffed. "And women who served as nurses in the war aren't allowed to receive military benefits."

"Even something as simple as serving on a jury isn't allowed for us," Nelly stated. "How can we ever have a fair trial with a jury of our peers when we are denied that right?"

"It's no wonder so many women turn to magic," Anna concluded with a heavy sigh.

As our drinks were served, we raised our glasses and made a toast. I asked Nelly to confirm that she called from Rose's and arranged for transportation.

"Of course," she replied confidently. "We'll head straight to the port."

I couldn't wait to see Claudia and make sure she was safe in this world again.

"And I'm prepared for a fight, if necessary," Olinda added.

"What do you mean?" Anna asked, her voice filled with worry.

As I took another sip of my drink, I felt a tightening grip around my heart. And suddenly, we're back in the present moment. We stepped back and then stepped forward again.

Pain shoots through my body, but it's mixed with a magical sensation. Olinda checks my vitals and confirms that I'm physically fine.

"My body is okay," I reassure my friends, who are looking at me with serious expressions. "But Claudia isn't. Something terrible has happened."

When we reach the train station, we stand by the door, ready to exit. As soon as the doors open, we rush out and make our way to the waiting car.

"How will we know which ship to go to?" Nelly asks.

She must be in shock because she should know the answer.

"The pain will increase, or you'll feel magic as we get closer," I explain.

"Why would we feel magic?" Anna questions. "Do Claudia and her friends practice magic too?"

"Not yet," I reply. "Their ship disappeared to another world, and I'm hoping, with Alex's help, they have returned to this one."

"What?" Olinda exclaims. "You knew all of this back at my house and didn't tell us? We could have helped."

"I'm sorry, but it's too late now," I say regretfully. "Please forgive me and let's focus on finding them."

"Well, you're feeling Claudia's pain because you're connected to her," Nelly speculates. "But what if Alex and the others are also hurt?"

"I should have packed medical supplies," Olinda laments.

The number of ships at the port is overwhelming. We walk and walk, but it seems like we're getting nowhere.

The tolling of bells echoes through the air, causing us all to turn towards the ship they're coming from. In that moment, I can't help but feel a pang of empathy for Claudia, realizing that if she had been standing in my place, she would have turned the wrong way due to her deafness. The ship would have been on her deaf side, and where the bells could only be heard on her hearing side. As I thought about this, a sudden wave of pain shot through my body.

"That's the ship," I exclaim, certain that it has to be the one we are looking for.

"You're right," Nelly confirms. "I can feel the magic emanating from it."

Claudia's deafness may have brought challenges, but it also gave her unique abilities. She could perceive things that others couldn't, picking up on subtle facial expressions and minute signs of body language.

As we rush towards the ship, I can sense Claudia's blood draining from her. Nelly leads our group, following the trail of magic until we reach the ship's entrance. We descend down a set of stairs and walk through a narrow hallway before arriving at a door. With Nelly leading the way, she opens it and what I see takes my breath away—Claudia pale as a ghost, her friends' fear etched into their features.

CHAPTER NINETEEN – CLAUDIA

"A knot for a tree
A tree for the fire
A fire in a stone
A stone in the soil"
Contributed by Archdruid Ellen Evert Hopman
Translation by Isolde Carmody

Marie's heart dropped as she fell to her knees at the sight of Claudia lying on the ground, a pool of blood forming around her injured body. Lina applied pressure with a clump of gauze from the ship's large first aid kit while Olinda joined in to assist.

"We need help," Olinda urgently called out to Nelly, who was quickly assessing the situation.

"Should we take her to the hospital?" Anna asked, her voice filled with worry.

"I'll call for an ambulance," Kiersten declared before sprinting out of the room and through the ship's hallway and stairs.

Meanwhile, Alex had not left Claudia's side, his tear-stained face hovering over hers. "You're going to be okay," he whispered, but she was unresponsive. He pressed his forehead against hers and wept. "Please don't leave me. I can't lose you."

In contrast, Marie remained frozen on her knees, like a statue carved from grief and sorrow. Her whole being felt imprisoned in this moment.

Claudia could feel herself slipping away, the life draining from her body despite her desperate struggle.

The sound of voices surrounded her, but she was too weak to open her eyes. She recognized Nelly's voice, asking about the men who had been handcuffed to the pipe earlier with an accusatory tone.

She caught glimpses of what happened after she was shot, but it was all a blurry haze in her mind.

As she drifted further into unconsciousness, a face appeared before her closed eyes. It wasn't the face she wanted to see—that of Alex or one of her friends—but that of a stranger. And yet, something about him felt familiar. His brow furrowed above sharp, unfeeling eyes and a pointed nose perched above a sad mouth and cleft chin.

"Do you remember me?" he asked in her delirious state.

"Who are you?" she questioned the stranger in her vision.

"My, you have lost a lot of blood. Your memories must be foggy. Let me help you," he offered with an eerie calmness.

Abruptly, visions of their journey flashed before Claudia's mind. They had jumped back in time on the S.S. Hewitt, only to be captured by Vernon, who had locked them up on board. In the midst of chaos, Vernon had punched Alex and then Kris showed up and shot him—or at least that's what Claudia was seeing through her delirium. The details were hazy, but it felt painfully real.

"What have you done?" Vernon barked at Kris, his anger palpable. "I didn't give you permission to shoot him."

Claudia's heart raced as she desperately tried to break free from the cold, metal shackles that bound her arms to the pipe. In front of her, Alex lay motionless on the ground as an officer placed two fingers on his neck and shook his head in confirmation. Claudia's worst fears were realized as the officers raised their guns and aimed them at her and her friends.

Florian was the first to fall, graceful even in her last moments. Lina followed, and with each gunshot, Claudia's heart shattered into a million pieces. Kiersten stood tall and gave the officers a fierce look, silently promising revenge from beyond the grave. And finally, it was Claudia's turn.

As she fell to the ground, pain ripping through her body, she looked up at the stranger standing over her. "Why?" she managed to gasp out.

"Just a little payback from another time," he replied coldly before darkness consumed her.

Kiersten burst into the room with a team of medics, frantically trying to save their friend. "She's been shot in the torso and is fading fast," Kiersten informed them.

The medics immediately went to work, assessing Claudia's condition. "She's unresponsive, but still breathing," one announced. "She's lost a lot of blood."

"We did our best to apply pressure to the wound," Lina added.

The medics nodded approvingly. "You did well. The bullet went completely through, so applying pressure was the right move. She could have also passed out from shock."

"We need to grab the stretcher and get her out of here," another medic instructed. "Keep pressure with this," he said before they departed.

Amidst all the chaos, Marie finally snapped out of her frozen state. "Ladies, we need a spell to extract Vernon's spirit," she said urgently.

"What are you talking about?" Vernon barked.

"I brought the shiny breast plate," Olinda interjected.

"Perfect. We can transfer his soul into the armor," Marie explained. The group quickly set to work, determined to save Claudia's life and bring justice to the ones who had wronged them.

Nelly's eyebrows furrowed in confusion as she asked, "Did you just say shiny armor?"

Marie chimed in, "Yes, like when you touched the collar during the reading. It's a good sign."

Olinda struggled to place the breast plate on Vernon, but he pushed back against her efforts.

"Stay still," Kiersten commanded, brandishing a letter opener in her hand. She pointed it at Vernon's neck with determination.

Olinda had an easier time securing the armor on Vernon the second time around. Once it was all in place, Marie led them through their chant, with even Lina and Kiersten joining in to speed up the spell's effects. Their voices in unison became a hum. A smoke like cloud floated above each chanter and then it swirled into Vernon's chest to extract the counter soul. Abruptly, Vernon jolted forward and demanded, "Who are you? Why am I handcuffed?"

"One of you," Marie waved her hand towards all the men secured to the pipe, "shot my daughter."

"It was him," Kiersten pointed an accusatory finger at Kris.

Vernon frantically searched his belt before realizing, "I can't find my keys. I need to get me and my officers free so we can arrest him."

Florian sheepishly took out a set of handcuff keys from her pocket and handed them to Vernon. The difference in his personality now that he had his own soul instead of a counter's was remarkable. He thanked her before freeing himself and moving onto the next officer.

Kris didn't take kindly to being arrested and attempted to resist by sliding down the pipe and headbutting the nearest officer. However, his attempt was futile as the officer simply headbutted him back, causing Kris to stumble and fall to the floor with his hands still cuffed to the pipe.

Once all of the officers were freed, they uncuffed Kris and escorted him out of the room.

The medics rushed in with a stretcher and placed it next to Claudia's limp body.

"We must hurry," one medic exclaimed urgently. "Time is of the essence."

The other medic's fingers were pressed against Claudia's neck as he assessed her condition. His hesitation was palpable as he struggled with what to say.

"Speak plainly and clearly," Marie demanded with a stomp of her foot, sensing the gravity of the situation.

"I don't think she's going to make it to the hospital," the second medic finally admitted, his voice filled with concern and regret.

"Why not?" Marie's voice rang out in panicked urgency.

"She's in need of immediate surgery and medicine, but she'll bleed out before we even reach the hospital." The first medic's words were clipped and rushed.

"But you can't know that for sure. Please, hurry!" Anna pleaded, her eyes wide with fear.

"Her heartbeat is alarmingly slow," Anna continued, her hand pressed to her own chest.

Marie looked around the room, her mind racing. How could they save her daughter in time?

"She's halfway across the room from you," Marie pointed out, furrowing her brow. "How can you possibly know her heartbeat?"

"I can feel it," Anna replied with conviction.

Marie stared at Anna in disbelief, while Florian, Kiersten, and Lina huddled closer to Claudia's side, calling out to her.

Alex leaned down and kissed Claudia's forehead gently, his face full of worry. "Please, wake up, Claudia."

Marie couldn't help but speak up. "What else do you feel?" She looked at Anna with curious eyes.

"She can hear all of you," Anna said quietly, her gaze never leaving Claudia's pale face.

"Really?" Kiersten asked in disbelief. Then she turned to Claudia and spoke directly to her. "I need you to give it your all. You can survive this."

"Come back to us, Claudia," Florian begged tearfully.

"We need you," Lina added desperately.

"I need you too," Alex whispered hoarsely.

"And I love you more than words can express, my dear daughter," Marie said, tears streaming down her face. "But your time here is far from over."

Claudia's eyes fluttered open slowly, causing a collective gasp from everyone in the room. They held their breath in anticipation, waiting for her to speak.

"How can it be?" the second medic asked in shock.

The first medic looked at Claudia's wound in disbelief. "It's healing. I've never seen anything like it."

"What happened?" Claudia croaked out, her voice weak but filled with curiosity.

"That, my dear, is a long story," Florian replied with a wide grin on her face. She was overjoyed to hear her friend's voice once again.

"You took a bullet for me," Alex spoke up, his eyes glistening with unshed tears. "You didn't need to do that. I would gladly have a bullet in me instead of you."

"Do you see now how much the boy loves your daughter?" Olinda asked Marie, a soft smile on her face.

"It's truly beautiful," Nelly added with awe in her voice.

"That's why you should be certain he reincarnates with her," Anna said, her voice weighted with urgency. "He shows all the signs that it will work. His spirit is open to the possibility, and they are true soulmates."

Marie turned to look at Anna, surprised by her sudden declaration. She was elated by Claudia's remarkable recovery and didn't understand the shift in conversation.

"What do you mean?" she asked, curious yet hesitant.

"Don't you see?" Anna pressed on. "With the additional timelines and counters, balance could potentially be restored."

Marie hesitated, unsure if this was truly the best course of action to defeat their enemy.

"And what harm could it possibly do?" Anna huffed, her tone bordering on impatience.

Marie noticed that Anna was clutching her sweater tightly against her stomach and looked paler than usual.

"Are you feeling all right?" Marie asked with concern.

"I'm fine," Anna reassured her, trying to brush off her unease. "I think I may just be getting seasick from being on this ship for so long."

"We need to get off this ship and find a safe place for you all," Marie said as she approached Claudia. "How are you feeling, my dear?"

Claudia gingerly touched her torso before sitting up slowly. "I think I'll survive," she said with a faint smile.

But before they could make any more plans or decisions, all of a sudden Anna collapsed onto the floor, gasping for air and clutching at her chest.

Panicked, Marie rushed over to her side, only to notice that blood was seeping through Anna's clothing in the exact spot where Claudia had been wounded earlier.

"What have you done?" Marie demanded, her heart racing with fear and confusion.

Anna let out a weak laugh as she struggled to speak. "Let's just say that I've learned a thing or two from being around you remarkable women: you, Olinda; you, Nelly; and you, Marie."

Nelly's fingers trembled as she pointed at the gaping wound on Anna's side. "But we never taught a spell to do that," she said, her voice filled with concern and confusion.

Anna's response was weak, her voice strained from pain. "During our time at Olinda's, I delved into a few books," she explained. "And I stumbled upon one of your journals, Marie." While everyone had been busy transferring the counter soul out of Vernon, she'd been busy transferring Claudia's injury to herself.

Marie's eyes widened in shock. "You what?"

"We'll need the eight of us this time, with the dual timeline in play," Anna continued. "If the counters grow stronger, reincarnation will no longer exist."

Lina's brow furrowed. "Wait, does that include us too?"

"What are you all talking about?" Claudia interjected, feeling left out of the loop.

"We'll explain later." Anna gasped, coughing up blood. "Right now, teach them the verbal poetry incantation."

"This is all *his* doing," Marie spat out angrily. "I knew he would come after both of you somehow."

Anna nodded weakly. "He's my lover throughout time, seeking revenge," she confessed. "This is my fault."

"Don't say that," Marie murmured, falling to her knees beside Anna and gently placing a hand on her cheek.

"I'm going to need some assistance," Florian spoke up from the corner of the room, identifying Anna's desire. Her natural ability as an empath ignited around all of the magic in the room. She knew Anna wanted the verbal poetry incantation to take place before it was too late. "I'm having trouble following everything, but I'm fascinated by it all."

"She's right," Marie agreed, wiping away tears from her cheeks. "Time is running out."

"Okay, Mother," Claudia conceded reluctantly. "Tell us what we need to do."

"Alex…" Anna turned her face toward him, her eyes searching his for an answer. "Are you okay with this? With living multiple lives with Claudia?"

Without hesitation, Alex replied, "Yes." Perhaps after witnessing the miracle that saved Claudia, and magical rings transporting an entire ship from another world, reincarnation didn't seem so far-fetched.

"Then please, take a seat in the center of the room," Marie instructed, nodding at Anna. "The rest of us will form a circle around you, including Anna where she lays."

Everyone followed Marie's lead, their hearts heavy with the thought of possibly losing Anna. But they were determined to carry out her final wish.

The verbal poetry incantation was spoken with love and life woven into every word. It pulled at emotions that people often bury deep inside, offering healing in a place free of judgment. It allowed anyone to live authentically, if only for one fleeting moment.

As the words filled the room, magic swirled and danced around them, touching each person's heart along the way. Claudia and Alex focused on their love for each other. Florian, Kiersten, and Lina thought of their unbreakable friendship. Olinda, Nelly, Anna, and Marie reflected on their indestructible bond as companions. The power of the verbal poetry enveloped them all, united by their shared experience and determination to fight against the forces trying to tear them apart.

Sisterhood. A bond that transcends time and space. In this moment, Marie and Anna felt their connection stronger than ever before. As the group stood together, Anna's eyes were opened to a vision of their past lives, their present selves, and even glimpses into their distant future. It was a swirling chaos of memories and possibilities.

Suddenly, Alex began to float a few inches off the ground before landing back with a *thud*. The group erupted in applause, but Marie rushed to Anna's side as she started to slip away.

"What can I do?" Marie cried out in desperation.

"Nothing." Anna gasped through her pain.

Marie felt her heart tighten like a vise once again. This cycle of reincarnation had begun when she lost her sister, and now she was losing her once more.

With tears streaming down her face, she cradled Anna's head in her hands. "I love you."

"I love you too." Anna's voice was barely audible. Time was running out. "I have a feeling we will meet again." She managed a weak smile before her head fell, a lifeless weight in Marie's hands. The cycle continued, but their love remained eternal.

CHAPTER TWENTY – ALEX

THE WALKER FAMILY
EXTENDS AN INVITATION FOR YOU TO ATTEND
A VISITATION IN HONOR OF
ANNA CHAMBERLAIN
ON THE EVENING OF FRIDAY
THE TWELTH OF FEBRUARY THE YEAR 1921
AT EIGHT O'CLOCK AT THE WALKER FAMILY
HOME

LET US CELEBRATE ANNA'S LIFE AND
ALL SHE GAVE TO THE COMMUNITY

The sound of Claudia's mother's cries echoed through the air, wrenching my heart. I had witnessed death before, but never in such a swift and intense manner. Claudia tightly embraced her mother as they both sought comfort from each other and their friends. Eventually, Claudia came to me, trembling with grief that she had been holding back for the sake of her loved ones. I held onto her firmly, offering whatever comfort I could in that moment.

Marie took charge once again, her voice steady and business-like as it had been during the search team meeting. "We still need to get everyone to safety," she stated. "We may have bought some time with Vernon and Kris, but I don't know how long it will last. There are new powers at play here."

She paused to clear her throat before continuing, "Olinda, can you please arrange for Anna to be transported back home? Nelly, we'll need to organize the grandest farewell party Kansas City has ever seen."

Lina stepped up to help Olinda, while Florian volunteered to assist Nelly. As a team now, I knew they would stop at nothing to make sure their plans were carried out successfully.

Kiersten hung onto every word Marie said, and the two of them engaged in a lengthy discussion. I could tell Kiersten was helping Marie hold back the crushing waves of grief that would inevitably hit. Despite her toughness and skill with a knife, she had a soft side that she often kept hidden.

"We have enough tickets for all of us to take the train back," Marie announced. "We should head to the station soon."

"I'm not sure where Vernon stashed the crate of birth control," Kiersten spoke up. "We need to find it before we can leave."

"Hopefully he was preoccupied with Kris and it's still on the ship," Marie replied calmly. "I'll help you search for it."

As we prepared to leave, I turned to Nelly and Florian and asked in a hushed tone, "Would it be possible for us to secure the booze that Vernon was moving?"

"I think we can manage that," Florian responded confidently.

Lina also quietly asked Kiersten, "Where did you locate the emergency crew? I'm hoping they can point us in the right direction for getting Anna safely moved."

First things first, we went to the medics to secure their assistance in preparing Anna. It was a delicate conversation to navigate, as we didn't want to draw attention after the miraculous event they had witnessed. I helped Lina find a phone so she and Olinda could call their contacts and arrange for everything that was needed.

Claudia's cheeks were slowly regaining their natural rosy hue, but she still appeared slightly fatigued. Her hair was tousled and disheveled, yet she remained breathtakingly beautiful. My heart swelled with gratitude that she was still alive.

"We'll need lotus flowers everywhere," Olinda's voice crackled into the phone. "Make sure to coordinate her outfit with the florist. I'll send over the details."

Nelly made a quick call about invitations, while Florian did the same to a different group. Everything seemed to be falling into place, as if the world was trying to make up for the heartbreak it had allowed on the ship.

But how long would this happiness and organization last? In my experience, balance rarely lasts for very long. As we made our way back to the ship, our tight-knit group stuck together, afraid of losing sight of anyone.

What seemed like hours passed as we searched through every nook and cranny of the cargo area, yet we were no closer to finding the birth control or booze.

"Where could that little devil have hidden it?" Nelly groaned in frustration.

"Do you think he took it with him when they took Kris?" Olinda speculated.

"But how would he explain that?" Marie interjected. "Blaming Kris for the booze is one thing, but he would have nothing to say about the birth control."

"Where was his room on this ship?" I turned to Claudia and her friends. "You spied on him, right?"

"Smart boy," Florian praised.

"Why didn't we think of that?" Lina sighed in annoyance.

"No time for regrets," Kiersten chimed in. "Follow me."

We marched past the kitchen and down a narrow hallway until Claudia abruptly froze.

"This is where it happened," she whispered.

"Yeah, where I removed Vernon's trigger finger," Kiersten jested.

"And where Claudia charged at him," Lina added with a shudder.

"That's when we were transported to another time," Claudia finished, her voice heavy with memories.

"Okay, ladies," Marie interrupted, her voice cutting through the air like a sharp knife. "You can tell us all about it during the train ride back home. Now, which one is his room?"

Kiersten eagerly pointed to a door further down the hall, her eyes sparkling with excitement.

As we opened the door and stepped inside, my senses were immediately overwhelmed by the sight and smell of countless boxes and barrels filling every inch of space in the small room. The dim light from a single window barely illuminated the chaotic scene before us.

Without hesitation, Kiersten and I began rummaging through the boxes, confirming their contents with each opening. As we worked, Marie explained that they had arranged for transportation to move everything from the dock and onto the cargo loading area of the train. We just needed to get everything off the ship.

"I saw hand trucks as we passed by the kitchen," Lina chimed in, always practical and observant.

With our task at hand, we quickly set to work moving boxes and barrels up the narrow stairs and out of the ship. The wooden plank I found proved to be a helpful tool in maneuvering items up the stairs.

Despite our heavy hearts over what we had lost, there was a sense of purpose and camaraderie amongst us as we worked together. And as we loaded everything onto trailers and boarded the train ourselves, exhaustion began to set in.

The long journey home was filled with somber silence as we reflected on our dear friend Anna's selfless actions that saved each one of us in some way or another. In her memory, Marie suggested ordering drinks from the train's bar carriage.

As glasses clinked together in a toast, each one of us shared stories and memories of Anna. Kiersten spoke of how she had been rescued from a raid before even meeting Anna. Florian toasted to Anna's impeccable taste and fashion sense. Lina praised Anna's business acumen and ability to break barriers for women. Claudia's voice trembled as she tearfully remembered how Anna had always put others before herself.

Finally, it was my turn to share my own story of how Anna had helped care for my sick ma and younger brother without ever passing judgment. And as I raised my glass to Anna, a mixture of gratitude and sorrow washed over me. She may be gone, but her selflessness and kindness would never be forgotten by those who loved her.

"Anna was the epitome of wisdom and kindness," Nelly said, lifting her glass in another toast. The crystal goblet gleamed in the light, casting a warm glow on the faces around me.

Olinda nodded in agreement. "She was unwavering and graceful, even in her last moments."

"I will always remember her dry humor. It could lift any mood," Marie added, wiping tears from her eyes. But then she frowned, lines forming on her forehead. "I should have brought the medics back while you did the incantation."

Olinda placed a comforting hand on Marie's arm. "It wouldn't have saved her. She was already beyond help, just like Claudia had been." She let out a heavy sigh. "And then we wouldn't have been able to fulfill Anna's final wish."

Marie took a deep breath and nodded solemnly. "To my sister throughout time!" She raised her glass, and we all clinked ours together before taking a sip.

After all of our previous activities, most of our group had drifted off to sleep. Only Claudia and I remained awake.

"Did you ever imagine we would end up here when we first met?" she asked, gazing at me with those bright eyes.

"I couldn't have fathomed it," I replied honestly, placing a hand on her knee. She leaned into my touch, her head resting on my shoulder.

"Who could have guessed?" She shrugged, a small smile playing on her lips.

"I never thought I'd face a gunshot directed at me, but you stopped it," I said softly.

"Yes, I did. And ultimately, it cost Anna her life."

I pulled Claudia closer into a hug. She shouldn't blame herself for something that was out of her control; Kris had been the one to pull the trigger.

"I also saw firsthand how skilled your friends are in combat," I said to her, earning a smile from Claudia. "I had no idea."

"Joining you in the fight for rights, seeing you blossom while giving a speech. So many experiences I wouldn't have had without meeting you," I continued, thinking back on all the adventures we'd been through together.

"And then you were knocked out after witnessing that speech," Claudia reminded me with a playful smirk.

"I'm pretty sure that would have happened whether I met you or not," I countered with a grin.

"Nope, it was because a couple of counters were following me, and I brought them closer to you."

"That wasn't your doing. It wasn't your fault," I reassured her.

"You're right," she conceded, leaning her head against my chest. And in that moment, surrounded by our close friends, I knew that I wouldn't want to be anywhere else but here with Claudia.

"If we'd never met, I'd never have had the chance to stay in a room with you all night aboard THE MISSOURI."

"Oh yeah, and we never would have kissed," she said playfully.

Claudia's hand reached up to gently brush my cheek, sending a wave of warmth through me. Our playful banter quickly turned into a passionate kiss, more fervent than the one we had shared onboard the ship. It was like we were making up for lost time and heartbreak.

Her fingers tangled in my hair as she pulled me closer. My hands found their way to the nape of her neck and down to the small of her back, pulling her body against mine. Claudia was intoxicating, and I wanted nothing more than to be with her in every sense.

We eventually broke away for air, both of us flushed and craving more. But despite our desire, I wanted to do things right.

"There is one thing I wish I could change," I whispered.

She leaned back slightly, mockingly surprised. "You'd change something about our disastrous relationship so far?"

"Yes," I said firmly, taking hold of her arms and pulling her back towards me. "I would have courted you properly instead of getting caught up in searching for a missing ship and becoming a reincarnated soul."

"You're okay with that last part, right?" she asked, searching my eyes.

I nodded, my heart swelling with love for this woman before me.

"Did someone say courting?" Lina quickly spoke up from her dazed state, her eyelids fluttering open.

"You must be dreaming." Kiersten chuckled, also awake now.

Florian's hands were clasped tightly together as she spoke. "We can plan the dates and outfits," she said with a renewed sense of her usual self, despite everything that had happened.

"We'll even chaperone," Nelly chimed in, letting us know they were all awake now.

"Of course, we can take turns," Olinda added.

"But not until my permission has been granted," Marie interjected, a sly smile on her face.

I turned to address her formally. "Marie Edwards Walker, it would be an honor if I could court your daughter."

Claudia's face lit up, and we all waited anxiously for Marie's response.

"Do you promise to always treat her with respect and protect her with everything you have?" Marie asked sternly.

"Mother, respect is important, but he can't promise to protect me with everything he has," Claudia retorted.

"I will do everything in my power to protect her," I answered firmly. "Even if it means taking a bullet for her, just like she did for me."

Claudia gasped loudly at my words. "No!"

"Let's hope we're never in that kind of situation again," I tried to reassure her.

"You have my permission," Marie finally said with a smile.

Florian was quick to chime in. "So it's settled then? You two are courting."

"Not so fast," I interrupted, turning back to Claudia. "The choice is yours."

Marie commended me for respecting Claudia's decision. "Yes, yes," Claudia agreed with a smile. "My answer is yes."

"That's settled then," Lina said excitedly. "Now we can focus on our plans for when we get home."

But Lina brought up a potential issue. "There may be a problem with Vernon remembering that we were moving illegal product."

"We can create a cloaking spell, at least for the product," Nelly offered.

"That could work," Olinda agreed.

"We'll make sure it lasts until it's delivered safely," Marie said confidently. "We don't want any problems."

"I also managed to get Frank, Thomas, and James to help me move the booze," I added.

Claudia's worried voice cut through the tense silence. "But won't Vernon remember that too?"

Marie's gentle tone rang out in response. "We'll cloak the booze as well."

Florian's smooth voice chimed in, breaking the tension. "Oh, be sure to remember to invite your friends to the Farewell Party. I'm sure Anna would have wanted them there."

My voice joined in, filled with excitement. "Of course, I'm sure they'd love to be there."

Kiersten's eager voice added to the discussion. "And I'll reach out to Athenaeum to invite John, Michael, and Arthur."

Claudia's determination was evident in her reply. "I can help with that."

Marie's disinterest caught me off guard. "We'll need to invite all of high society. It would be expected for such an event."

A disinterested grunt escaped Claudia, much to my delight.

"We should also invite everyone from Anna's resort," I suggested.

"Of course, as well as your ma and brother," Marie said dutifully.

Lina summarized our plans with a confident nod. "Sounds like everything is set."

The train jostled and rattled on its tracks as we continued our journey. Gathering in a circle, we clasped hands and recited the cloaking spell Nelly had taught us. Surrounded by the warmth of my friends' hands and the strength of their magic, I couldn't believe how far I had come since meeting Claudia. If someone had told me this would be my life before, I never would have believed them.

Armored Hours

Chapter Twenty-One
Marie

Armored Hours

Two immaculately dressed attendants stand at attention next to the towering columns that frame the grand entrance to the Walker Family home—my home. With crisp, white gloves, they meticulously check each person against the carefully curated guest list as they enter. Every detail has been arranged with precision and perfection, a fitting tribute to my dear sister, Anna. In truth, she deserved so much more, but this is the best I could do.

As I step inside, my senses are immediately overwhelmed by the elegant beauty of the ballroom. A central fountain is adorned with floating lotus flowers, their petals a perfect match for the delicate fabric draping the two-story windows around the room. Each window is tied back with satin bows that catch the light from the glittering chandeliers above. Even Anna's burial dress echoes this color scheme, a tribute to her presence at this event.

The room is filled with finery and opulence, and a string quartet plays a heavenly tune in the background. Memories flood my mind as I take in the scene before me, memories of my sister and me as children before all of this began. We used to play with a hand-carved spinning top, our laughter filling the air as we made it spin faster and faster.

But now, it's time to return to the present. So many people have gathered here tonight to honor Anna's memory. Even Dorothy and Rose are here. They mingle and drink from delicate crystal flutes or decanters, sharing happy anecdotes and memories of her. I make my way through the crowd, greeting Alex and his friends first.

"Allow me to introduce you to Marie Walker, Claudia's mother," Alex says graciously.

"It's a pleasure to meet you," one of the men responds shyly, glancing around at the others before taking a sip from his glass.

Alex introduces each of them in turn—Frank, who compliments our lovely home and James, whose handshake reveals callouses from hard work. "Thank you for being here, Frank and James," I reply with a warm smile.

"And I am Thomas, Madam," the third boy says with a warm smile that seems to radiate with joy and laughter. "Anna's resort was one of the finest I have ever seen. She invited us for dinner once and treated me as an equal, never once looking down on me because of my humble background. I'm blessed to have known her."

His words are sweet and sincere, moving my heart with their honesty. "I appreciate your kind words. Anna always valued hard work and a kind heart."

"She had such a gracious spirit," James adds. "She paid her employees far more than her competitors ever did."

I can't help but smile, knowing that this description perfectly fits my sister.

"Yes, she was always compassionate towards others," Frank chimes in.

"Thank you," I tell them sincerely.

Alex swiftly opens his arms for a hug, and I find myself gratefully accepting it. His embrace is warm and comforting, exactly what I need in this moment.

"Please enjoy yourselves," I say before moving on to greet the next group.

Florian and Kiersten stand together with a few men from the Athenaeum, who I assume are business associates.

"Hello, dear ones," I say warmly to Florian and Kiersten. "Will you introduce me?"

"Marie, this is John," Florian points out a young man with a boyish grin.

"And this is Michael," Kiersten says while placing her hand on another man's shoulder.

"It's a pleasure to meet you," he says with a charming smile. "I must say, your headpiece is absolutely stunning."

"Thank you," I respond graciously, gently touching the intricate headpiece borrowed from Anna's belongings.

"I'm Arthur," the third man introduces himself. He has a rugged appearance, with a crooked nose that looks like it has been broken multiple times. But despite his tough exterior, he exudes warmth and friendliness.

"It's lovely to meet all of you," I say sincerely.

"Anna always welcomed us with open arms," Arthur says, his voice catching with emotion. "We can never repay her now." He sniffles slightly.

"What if I told you there may be a way for you to do just that?" I ask, looking directly at Florian and Kiersten.

"Just name it," Kiersten responds without hesitation.

"Well, you see, Anna left behind the resort."

Florian clasps her hands together excitedly while letting out a squeal of delight.

"I haven't even shared the plans yet," I say with a small laugh. And so I proceed to tell them the details as I announce it to the rest of the room. Claudia and her friends would all be equal partners in the venture. Kiersten would oversee the kitchen and bar, Florian would handle decorating and wardrobe, Lina would handle business and accounting, Claudia would work on securing investors and lobbying efforts with Nelly and Olinda, Alex and his friends would assist with construction and supplies, and the Athenaeum gentlemen would serve as protection for the property.

Anna's employees all smile when I say the resort will continue to provide them with tools to control their own fate.

"That is how Anna will never be forgotten," I close and the entirety of the people there weep and clap their hands.

I finally go to where my sister lies. Claudia, Lina, Olinda, and Nelly are there too, knowing I wouldn't want to be alone.

"She looks beautiful and at peace," Nelly says.

Olinda puts her arm around me. Claudia holds my hand while Lina has her arm around her. I look at my sister and Nelly was right. Anna looks beautiful and at peace. I reach into the casket and hold her hand.

I'm instantly hit with a scene from the very distant future without vegetation. My sister in this distant future stands before me. She has rosy cheeks, but I haven't seen this before. I know it's her, though. I can feel it. Then my other hand tingles. It's the one Claudia holds. She's sharing her vision with me. I guess that means she's able to see the future and the past like me now too.

How did that happen? And then, I'm back in the vision. My sister looks deep into my eyes as if she can read my thoughts. She pats my shoulder.

"There, there, Marie. Things will feel normal here before you know it," she says with a warm nod.

My heart swells from feeling her touch, even if it is only in a vision. Seeing my sister is so sweet. I'm thankful to Claudia. The tingle returns, and I'm thrown into another scene. This one is from a nearer future, but in the alternate realm. Just like the previous scene, my sister of the time is in front of me again.

"There, there, you two. I'm proud of both of you and love you to pieces," she says and hugs Claudia and me.

Tears run down my cheeks unrelentingly now. My sister offers words of comfort through all the timelines. My hand tingles once more. Bright light filters in, and Anna stands before me.

"Sister, don't cry," she says.

"But it's so hard without you."

"Never forget. We will meet again."

She smiles, and my tears stop. She's right. This is not the last time we will see each other.

And just like that, I'm back at the party.

"Friends, will you give me a moment with my daughter?" I ask Nelly, Olinda, and Lina.

"Of course," Lina says. She hugs Claudia and walks to join Kiersten and Florian.

My friends nod and find their way to mingle among the crowd.

"How are you able to see past and future now?" I ask Claudia as soon as everyone's out of earshot.

"I'm not sure. It happened after I nearly died."

"Well, that is something."

"And you can see it too? Have you always?" she asks.

"Yes."

"Why didn't you tell me?"

"I didn't want to burden you."

"I am not a child anymore," Claudia defends.

"I know."

"Well, what do you plan to do next?" she questions.

"What do you mean?"

"About Anna's—your sister's lover throughout time."

"We took his soul out of Vernon and placed it into magical, shiny armor. And, Vernon locked up Kris. The counters have been taken care of."

"Is that what you think?" Claudia had released my hand when our friends gave us privacy, but she takes it again now and the tingling is immediate.

We are once again in the very distant future, but viewing the future Claudia now. I don't know how I know, but she's telepathically speaking to my sister's love throughout time. In this very distant future, he's cruel beyond words. He tortures people, and Claudia's forced to bear witness and experience it firsthand. She telepathically sends visions of him being tortured instead of it being the other way around.

I understand this justice and feel extremely proud of my daughter to have the strength for it. As the images assault my sister's lover's mind, I watch him suffer. He finally succumbs to a heart attack, and I witness my daughter's will break a little. She feels like she's committed murder when she's tried so hard to be on the right side of things.

"This wasn't your fault," I console Claudia.

"Keep watching," she says and squeezes my hand.

Now we're watching the soul of my sister's lover as he plans and colludes with power and time itself. Which brings us to our dual timelines and the counters.

"You see, it is all my fault, which is why I will fix this," Claudia says.

"It's not your fault," I argue.

"Nevertheless, I know how to resolve it."

"How?"

"I must go to where this all began."

The string quartet begins a new song, and footsteps can be heard behind us.

"Excuse me," Alex says. "May I borrow your daughter for a dance?"

Claudia turns around. "Of course. Right, Mother?"

All I'm able to do is turn around and nod.

Alex takes Claudia's hand and leads her to the dance floor around the fountain. They dance as only soulmates can. Anna was right to add Alex to our reincarnated family.

Olinda and Nelly join me.

"Ladies, I'm going to need another spell."

"Which one?" Nelly asks.

"A protection spell."

"Maple leaves should help for that," Olinda provides.

"But we need to collect oak for Claudia," Nelly interjects.

That makes perfect sense. Oak assists travel. I take a step toward Claudia, but Olinda grabs my arm.

"You knew," I accuse them of what I already know to be true.

"She's ready," Nelly says. "Just look at her."

Claudia and Alex dance perfectly to the rhythm of the music. They look like angels on the dance floor. I wish my sister could see it.

"She's not going alone," I tell them.

"Of course not," Olinda agrees.

"You'll need enough oak to include me," I say.

"But we're already collecting for two plus now maple for you," Nelly says.

"Who's the second?" I ask.

"Him," Olinda says. "He's her soulmate."

Just then Claudia kisses Alex and it's as if literal fireworks go off in my house. Lights flicker, the water in the fountain raises, and all heads turn their way.

"They both hold magical power within themselves," Nelly says.

They do, and I believe they can handle this next task, but I will still go with them to help. And my sister will be there to help too.

EPILOGUE – CLAUDIA

DEAR JOURNAL
I KNOW IT'S BEEN A LONG TIME
MUCH HAS OCCURRED
I'VE FOUND LOVE
WE'VE ENDURED LOSS
NOW WE GO ON A JOURNEY
CLAUDIA

As our fingers intertwine, I feel a sense of completeness and contentment that only comes when Alex is by my side. It's more than just practical necessity. It's a spiritual need and desire that could consume me entirely.

We're out in the woods gathering oak for Nelly and Olinda to build a magical threshold. This will be our portal to another time, a sacred passageway. Originally, I had planned to go alone, but Alex insisted on joining me.

It became clear to me that something had to be done to stop the dual timeline when a bullet narrowly missed him. I worry now about the danger he could be putting himself in by coming with me.

"What are you thinking about?" Alex picks a stray leaf off my clothes and places a comforting hand on my shoulder.

"Nothing," I say with a smile, lost in his piercing gaze. There have been countless moments where I've fallen deeper in love with him.

"Oh, come on," he teases, moving his hand to the nape of my neck. "I can see those wheels turning."

"Just about how lucky I am to have you by my side," I admit, placing my hands on his hips.

"Uh huh, so you weren't thinking about how dangerous this trip might be for me?" he asks softly, pressing his forehead against mine. "Trying to come up with a plan to keep me here while you go off gallivanting alone?"

"How do you do that? Read my mind?" I ask playfully, leaning closer to him. "And I wouldn't call it gallivanting."

"I know." He leans in for a kiss as I wrap my arms around him. Pure bliss fills every inch of my being. The only downside to this new adventure is that it will disrupt the peaceful time we've had together these past few days. But I couldn't risk letting the counters or the dual timeline find another way to harm us.

"Ahem," Kiersten interrupts as she approaches. "How much maple did Olinda say we needed to collect?"

Alex and I reluctantly pull away. "I'm not sure," I say, hoping she'll leave so we can continue kissing.

Kiersten quips with a raised eyebrow and laughter, "You're not sure, or his lips made you lose brain cells?"

Peering into Kiersten's basket, Lina declares, "We need a bushel. You're almost there."

As Florian skips over to join them, she asks in jest while inspecting our baskets, "How much oak have you two lovebirds managed to collect? Tsk, tsk, looks like someone's distracted."

Thomas, Frank, and James join the group, comparing baskets and engaging in friendly competition like siblings. It brings a smile to my face to see their camaraderie and know they'll have each other's backs if I am unable to return.

"You're going to need to increase the ingredients enough for three," Mother announces as she appears from around the corner.

Surprised, I ask, "What are you doing here? And what's this about ingredients for three?"

"I'm going with you, of course," Mother replies matter-of-factly.

Taking her hands in mine, I say warmly, "You know that I can do this, right?"

"Yes, you can," she affirms. "But I'm not passing up the opportunity to see my sister and your father. Well, I guess it's a different version of them, but they'll still feel like family."

I see the tears glistening in her eyes and feel torn. I don't want to put another person in danger, but it's hard not to give in to her desire. She has lost so much; no wonder she wants to go.

"Wait, I get to see Father?" I ask incredulously.

"Yes, won't that be nice?" Mother says with a smile as she wraps an arm around me. It's settled; she's coming with us.

After bringing our baskets into Olinda's home, we sit down at the table for a proper meal prepared by Nelly. The warmth and comfort of being surrounded by my loved ones gives me strength for the journey ahead.

I remember first meeting Alex at the ball, hiding away in a storage room with my rebellious crew. He had tentatively earned our trust that day, and our bond has only grown stronger since then. Looking at him now, I can't help but smile; his entire face seems to light up in response. I am a lucky woman.

Florian, Kiersten, Lina, and I have been through so much together. I couldn't imagine going through it all with anyone else. These friends are like the sisters I never had. In this moment, Florian flicks her wrist to show Kiersten a new bracelet. Kiersten playfully feigns excitement, hand to her forehead and neck bent back. Lina rolls her eyes, but a half-smile tugs at the corner of her mouth.

Mother's friends have also been a strong foundation for me. They will support each other through thick and thin, just like my own friends and I. We are all strong suffragettes united in our cause.

The bond between Alex, Frank, James, and Thomas is unbreakable also. Each man carries the weight of a tragic past, working tirelessly as bootleggers to provide for their loved ones. Yet, they still find time to help us in our mission.

As we finish dinner, Olinda's voice rings out from the kitchen. "Everything is ready. It's all set up in the back."

We quickly clean up and follow her outside to the backyard.

"Did you bring it?" Olinda asks my mother eagerly.

"Of course," my mother replies, pulling a worn leather journal from the bag slung over her shoulder.

"What's that?" I ask, curious.

"It's my journal from 1649," my mother replies with a hint of amazement in her voice. "Can you believe it has been preserved all this time?"

"Whoa," Lina exclaims. "How did you track down its location?"

"My journal ended up in a small-town museum in Virginia. I located it a few years ago and kept it safe at home, never imagining it would be used for this purpose."

"That's fascinating," Frank adds.

"Unfortunately, I could only secure this one. But luckily, it's the exact one we need."

Olinda turns to Thomas, Frank, and James. "Please join Nelly at the basket of maple leaves. She will guide you through the protection spell."

"The rest of you, come with me for the travel spell."

We follow Olinda's instructions, gathering around the candles and under the light of the moon.

Our plan is to prevent my aunt's lover from reincarnating so that he can't cause any further turmoil. Though it seems he has already caused quite a bit of damage in his previous life.

Burning some oak clears the air and creates a magical portal door.

"Awen," Olinda instructs Mother, Alex, and me. "That's what you will say as you circle your arms around the smoke from the fire or a candle, whichever calls to you."

I choose the larger fire, its smoke more visible and alluring. Olinda walks us through forming the shape of three circles forming a triangle with the smoke.

"Now repeat 'Awen' three times."

We are so close now. The fear that had been threatening to consume me pushes against my will once again. But I have faith in my mother's plan. It will put an end to the counters and dual timeline.

What worries me is that even if Vernon's interference is removed, he will still be a persistent cop who will pursue us for illegal substances. And Kris, well, he will still be Alex's competition in every sense of the word. His run-in at Anna's did not seem to have anything to do with counters or dual timelines. So, I need to somehow warn Anna in her past life and hope she can be saved.

As the spell nears completion, I look at our friends and say, "Until we meet again, Awen." And with that, Mother, Alex, and I vanish into thin air.

THE END

ACKNOWLEDGMENTS

Armored Hours exists today because of an incredible network of support and collaboration. I am filled with immense gratitude, even though words cannot fully express it. Nonetheless, I will attempt to convey my appreciation here.

A huge thank you to the brilliant minds who shared their creativity and organization skills, and supported this book's journey in countless ways: Kelly Allenby, James Young, Caroline Trussell, and Amy Brewer. Their ideas, inspiration, and advice have been invaluable.

I am also grateful to the communities and medical teams who have guided me through my journey with deafness. About a year before writing this novel, I experienced a ruptured eardrum in my non-deaf ear. During treatment, a cyst was discovered in my brain. Six months before the pre-order went live, another cyst was found but the first one had shrunk. With your ongoing guidance and support, we continue in search of answers.

Lastly, thank you to my children for their unwavering belief in me and their limitless love. When I write about a mother's love, I draw from the beautiful experience of being your mother. I am fortunate to have such awesome children like you in my life.

ABOUT THE AUTHOR

Stephanie Hansen is a PenCraft and Global Book Award Winning Author as well as an Imadjinn finalist. Her debut novella series, *Altered Helix*, released in 2020. It hit the #1 New Release, #1 Best Seller, and other top 100 lists on Amazon. It is now being adapted to an animated story for Tales. Her debut novel, *Replaced Parts*, released in 2021 through Fire & Ice YA and Tantor Audio. It has been in a Forbes article, hit Amazon bestseller lists, and made the Apple young adult coming soon bestsellers list. The second book in the *Transformed Nexus* series, *Omitted Pieces*, released in 2022. Her debut spicy paranormal romance, *Ghostly Howls*, released 2023. She is a member of the deaf and hard of hearing community, so she tries to incorporate that into her fiction. https://www.authorstephaniehansen.com/

DON'T MISS BOOK TWO IN THE REINCARNATED SOULS SERIES: GUARDED TIME

HTTPS://WWW.AUTHORSTEPHANIEHANSEN.COM/